D1760396

FRANKIE ABBOTT'S
GREAT BIG
BOOK OF
HORROR STORIES

BAINTE DEN STOC

WITHDRAWN FROM DÚN LAOGHAIRE-RATHDOWN
COUNTY LIBRARY STOCK

Edited by

David Barry

Frankie Abbott's Great Big Book of Horror Stories
Published in 2021 by
Acorn Books
www.acornbooks.co.uk

Acorn Books is an imprint of
Andrews UK Limited
www.andrewsuk.com

Copyright © 2021 David Barry

The right of David Barry to be identified as the author
of this work has been asserted by him in accordance
with the Copyright, Designs and Patents Act 1988.

All rights reserved. No reproduction, copy or transmission
of this publication may be made without express prior
written permission. No paragraph of this publication may be
reproduced, copied or transmitted except with express prior
written permission or in accordance with the provisions of the
Copyright Act 1956 (as amended). Any person who commits
any unauthorised act in relation to this publication may be
liable to criminal prosecution and civil claims for damage.

All characters appearing in this work are
fictitious. Any resemblance to real persons,
living or dead, is purely coincidental.

For Stuart and Jen at Misty Moon

Contents

Foreword by Frankie Abbott

Deer Reader, I hope you will enjoy these frightning storys, the ones I told to David Barry. I know I shoudn't say this, but he was allways trying to go one better than Hank Abbott. I mean, these was my storys and he knicked them. I come up wiv far better gory stuff than he done, but the trouble was somefink to do wiv the publishers who wanted good grammer and no spelling mistakes. But these was still my stories, and I fink him knicking them is called somefink like playgerism. I couldave sue'd him, but I offerd to let him off cos he give me loadsa money to buy chips an' stuff. Here is what our working reelationship was like.

The first day I come up wiv a revolting story about slugs — cos they is revolting — and he immediatly starts typing, but when he reads back wots written, it were nothink like wot I tells him. When I dictatid it to him, I had an exploding teddy bear that was an ingenias invention made by the slugs — who are really aliens in disguise — and they wants to unleash a deadly nervous gas to wipe out the world unless a ransom of twenty billion dollars is payed into a secret bank account on a distant planet.

But none of that got in my slugs story. At first I throws a wobbly, threatens to burn his hair off if he dont write wot I tells him. But he just laughs and gives me some gelt (witch is money) to go out an' get whatever nosh I fancies. So I come back wiv burger, chips, batterd sausage, mushy peas, a huge tub of Tom and Jerrys ice cream, a bar of Snickers, Maltesers, a big bag of M&M's and a two litter bottle of Fanta. And then he starts moaning cos I only give him two pee change from the twenty quid he give me.

It was like that every day for weeks. I come up wiv great stories like the vampire nuns who worked as undercover call girls, and he give that one the elbow an all. Then there was one about aliens who land on earth and only eat the hands and feet of humans cos they reckons they are a delicacy, and they must eat them while they are still alive, but they are not monsters, cos they provide the hand and foot eaten humans wiv artificial limbs. But it turns out bad cos these limbs is made of a sugery substance and attracts killer bees who sting them to death.

I thought that was me best story, but I was realy annoyed when he give it the elbow. But in the end, some of my bestest ideas got into the book, and when he told me I could make some money for it, I began to let him off what I would do to him if he didn't toe the line. I says to him, 'Listen you rat faced fink, I might have to put you on my hit list. One day you'll be walking along the road and the lights'll go out. A high-power rifle wiv a silencer will do the trick. You wont feel a thing but it'll be curtains all the same. That will teach you to mess wiv F.A.'s brilliant storys.'

But in the end I think we both come up wiv a good horrific read, although I think you might've guess it was FA wot done the hard graft. And if I write another book of horror stories, it will be a classic. That I can promise you, on me teddy's life. And I will definitely have vampire nuns as undercover call girls. Don't know why, but that realy appeals to me.

So next time you goes in a bookshop and sees a cover with a nun, dripping blood from her fangs and showing a leg in a fishnet stocking, you can bet your sweet teeth that F.A. has been using his loaf once more.

So, please look forward to one day reading about vampire nuns. As long as it doesn't become a habit! Geddit? Just one of Frankie's little jokes.

But for now, enjoy reading the storys what I imagined and told to David.

Frankie Abbott
October 2021

FRANKIE ABBOTT'S
GREAT BIG
BOOK OF
HORROR STORIES

1: The Great Lucifer

William Corbett of the Corbett Private Enquiry Agency was bored. He chewed the end of his electronic cigarette, his tongue running along the indented grooves of the plastic mouthpiece as he attempted to concentrate on writing another tedious surveillance report for an organisation who had hired him to observe their employees, which he had diligently done, and found nothing amiss, and therefore very little of interest to report.

He sighed deeply and blew out a non-carcinogenic stream of vapour and stared wistfully at his CCTV screen, hoping a beautiful blonde client would appear outside his door at any moment, wanting his services to track down some missing jewellery or top-secret plans for the latest cyber weapons of mass destruction. He knew it was a forlorn hope, brought about by viewing too many black and white movies on his home cinema screen. No one watched those anymore. He hadn't met a single person who had seen any film dating back earlier than 2020.

As his eyelids began to droop, he thought he could feel a sudden rush of air as he heard the elevator leaving the ground floor and he was suddenly alert, anticipating the striking entrance of that beautiful blonde client. In my dreams, he thought, wondering if the elevator would stop at the floor below his to offload a handful of unremarkable clients for the Drone Insurance Company. And then he heard the ping of the lift, signalling its arrival at floor eight – his floor! – followed by the robotic voice informing any sight-impaired passengers they had reached their intended destination.

Corbett stared at the screen as the door slid open, and out waddled a man of about fifty years-old, overweight and balding, his shoulders hunched from an invisible yoke of depression. The elevator doors clanged shut behind him, and Corbett could see on the screen how vulnerable and lost the man looked as he gazed up at the vestibule camera, wondering what to do next.

To put the man out of his misery, Corbett quickly depressed the button on his metal desk and stood up with a welcoming smile as the office door slid silently open.

'Please. Come in, come in,' he said, and gestured to a chair.

The man shuffled forward uncertainly. When he noticed the door closing automatically behind him, his head spun back like a startled animal.

Corbett chuckled, hoping to put the man at ease, and nodded to the chair. The man seemed to recover from his initial nervousness and lowered himself into the chair. Corbett opened a drawer and took out his electronic tablet, tapped the screen and prepared to take notes. 'First of all,' he began, 'can I take your name?'

The man cleared his throat quietly before speaking. 'My name is Callas. Jolyon Callas.'

'Well, Mr Callas, what can I do for you?'

'It's my son,' stammered the potential client. 'He's disappeared.'

Corbett tapped the 'Missing Person' logo on the screen, then raised an enquiring eyebrow at Callas. 'Name?'

The man stared vacantly at him, as if in a state of shock.

'What is your son's name?'

'Oh, yes, I see… My son's name was Robert Callas.'

Corbett stopped tapping the screen. 'You said "was". Why is that?'

'Because I think something terrible may have happened to him. How can a fairly well-known actor just disappear?'

Corbett had never heard of him, but he didn't say so. 'Your son was an actor?'

Callas nodded sadly. 'One of the best.'

'Hmm,' mused Corbett. 'Difficult times for an actor. Most TV and films these days use computer generated models instead of actors.'

'My son was one of the luckier ones,' Callas mumbled. 'He was extremely handsome, *and* he was a good actor. He was doing all right for himself. Until he joined the Great Lucifer's company.'

'The magician?'

'I think he likes to be known as an illusionist. Have you seen his show?'

'I can't say I have.'

Callas shuddered. 'I have, and it's disgusting. My son always said that people these days would only return to the theatre if one gave them public hangings. He was right.'

'Was the Great Lucifer your son's last employer?'

Callas nodded. 'Yes, a month ago my son was offered a job with the Great Lucifer. I don't hold with those sorts of shows and I didn't want him to do it.

But, you see, the Great Lucifer offered my son more money in a week than he normally earned in a month. The Great Lucifer can afford it.'

'His shows are certainly popular,' Corbett agreed. 'When did your son last get in touch?'

'About three weeks ago. He emailed me to tell me about accepting the engagement. But when I telephoned the Great Lucifer's theatre a week later and asked to speak to Robert, I was told he had left the show. Walked out, they said. But something – I don't know what it was – made me disbelieve them. So, I went to see the show for myself. How I sat through two hours of that disgusting spectacle I'll never know. But I did. And my son wasn't in it. He seems to have disappeared.'

Corbett felt a tremor of excitement as he thought of the far more compelling investigation that was within his reach, though he concealed his feelings with a deadpan expression.

'I would like to undertake this investigation,' he said. 'But I must warn you that it won't be – um – how shall I put it? – inexpensive. I think I ought to start by seeing the Great Lucifer's show, and the tickets, I believe, may only be obtained on the black market.'

Callas fished an envelope out of his pocket and handed it to the detective. It contained a thousand pounds and a ticket for the front row of the dress circle. Corbett looked up, suspiciously.

'This ticket is for tonight. How could you be so sure I would accept the job?'

'I suppose,' Callas answered sadly, 'I just hoped.'

***

The driverless cab Corbett took to the theatre that night only took him so far; he had to walk the last quarter of a mile as no traffic was permitted to enter the Leisure Square Mile. The detective pressed his hand on to the cab's fare VDU, the robotic voice thanked him for using their services, then the automatic door slid open and he stepped out into the teeming streets.

Shouldering his way along the busy thoroughfare, Corbett was glad he rarely had to visit this area. It was almost impossible to shuffle at more than a snail's pace along the overcrowded streets, and the dazzling neon and blaring music was punishing. Overhead a surveillance drone hovered, and Corbett not for the first time wondered how any person might be singled out for monitoring, and guessed the drones were used for alerting the Guardians of Peace to any disturbances.

It had been many years since the detective had visited one of the few remaining early twentieth century theatres, and he felt a sentimental pang of nostalgia for a past he had never known as he approached the sumptuous building. But the hardened detective soon recovered from his schmaltzy indulgence, knowing his mission was merely observational groundwork for his missing person quest.

As he took his seat in the dress circle, he was glad he had allowed himself plenty of time to get to the theatre and saw he was one of the first to arrive. He was keen to discover the sort of people who came to see an evening of macabre conjuring tricks. But as the auditorium filled it became clear to him that here was a great cross section of society, who was – like himself – merely curious. However, as it neared time for the curtain to rise he could feel a sense of communion running through the audience, united in their expectations of experiencing something fearful. Then, without warning, the auditorium was suddenly plunged into darkness and the hubbub of the crowd was switched off like a light. And from the stage came an eerie, high-pitched note. Slowly a spotlight began to fade-up on stage. Standing in the beam was a giant of a man, wearing a Mephistophelean beard and robes of fine silk.

Corbett almost sniggered superciliously. It was a cheap trick, using high decibel electronic music to cover the sound of the curtain rising, and a total black-out instead of a slow dim. He sat through the first half of the show feeling slightly superior and cynical as he watched the old-hat illusionist's tricks of sticking swords through women in coffin-shaped boxes. The only difference with these tricks was the fact that the performers simulated agonised screeches, and the swords were withdrawn covered in blood and gore. Gruesome, thought Corbett. But still old-hat.

The second half, though, was more frightening. A guided tour of torture through the ages. And some of the actors were so chillingly real that even the world-weary detective felt nauseated. But after each physical torment, there was always the incongruity of the recovered performers, smiling and bowing energetically like circus tumblers.

And even the cynical detective had to admit that the climax of the evening was stunning and a masterpiece of Grand Guignol theatre. The scene was the gallows, and the Great Lucifer passed sentence on an unhappy-looking actor.

A drum began to beat as the actor climbed the scaffold. He looked genuinely worried about the illusion, as if afraid it might not work. As the noose was tightened around his neck, he glanced into the wings. Then, as if he had been cued from offstage, he let out a terrifyingly realistic, blood-curdling scream. The executioner took hold of the lever. The actor appeared to be trying to say something, to speak directly to the audience, but the drum beat louder, smothering his remonstrations. The Great Lucifer made an imperious gesture and the hangman pulled the lever. The drum stopped as the actor's body hurtled through the trapdoor, and the audience gasped as they heard the vertebrae snap as the body reached the end of the rope.

The corpse was then cut down and placed in a coffin, brought on by four pallbearers. The lights dimmed, and the Great Lucifer made theatrical gestures while muttering unintelligible incantations over the coffin. Suddenly, the lid flew off and the audience jumped. The actor leaped out and pranced about the stage, bowing and smiling. The Great Lucifer permitted himself a smile. It had all been a delightful joke. Relieved, the crowd laughed, and the applause thundered as the illusionist took dozens of curtain calls.

Although Corbett didn't think the show was really his cup of tea, theatrically he couldn't deny its effect on the audience, and indeed himself. On his way home, he was so engrossed in trying to work out how the illusions worked, he almost forgot his reason for the visit to the theatre. When he remembered, he dashed indoors and sent an email to the Great Lucifer's company, applying for a job as a performer. He took the precaution of using a brand-new email address and adopted a pseudonym.

***

The next day, while Corbett breakfasted, he sank once again into his usual early-morning despondency. His wife had left him for another man two years ago, and though he rarely missed her, he often felt a desperate loneliness early in the day when he would have liked to share his investigative problems with someone. But now that he had what looked like an interesting case to work on, he soon overcame his low spirits and began his research into Robert Callas's disappearance.

First, he telephoned his client, to find out who the young actor's friends were. But after dozens of phone calls he drew a blank. No one seemed to know what had become of Robert Callas, and the trail appeared to end at the Great Lucifer's company. By late afternoon, after many enquiries, Corbett was convinced the young actor's disappearance had something to do with the illusionist's company. All he could do now was wait.

Then, just as he was about to abandon hope of getting a response to the email he had sent to the Great Lucifer's company, he received a reply from the illusionist himself, offering him an audition the very next day. The email was concise to the point of saying nothing other than the time and place. But at least, Corbett thought, it would give him an opportunity to secretly invade the enigmatic illusionist's territory where he might discover what had happened to his client's son.

***

Early the following morning Corbett waited his turn to see the illusionist, along with a dozen other men and women. When his turn eventually came, he was summoned into the grubby rehearsal studio. The Great Lucifer sat expansively in a throne-like chair which was raised on a small rostrum.

Corbett suddenly experienced a weird sensation. Had he met the illusionist somewhere before? He was certain he hadn't, because he had almost total recall when it came to putting names to faces. Yet the illusionist's face seemed all too familiar; lined and twisted, like the face from an old engraving. And his eyes were not living eyes. They were like glass, cold and soulless.

He stood nervously in front of the illusionist, waiting for the man to speak. The Great Lucifer stared for a long time at Corbett before speaking, aware of the dramatic effect he created. When he eventually spoke, his voice echoed in the studio.

'Your name is Irving. Not Henry Irving?'

'No,' Corbett replied. 'Harry Irving.'

Lucifer's lips stretched into the semblance of a smile, though his eyes lacked any trace of warmth.

'Please hand the email you were sent to my assistant.'

Corbett fumbled in his jacket pocket and handed the folded sheet of paper to one of Lucifer's minions.

'Now,' the illusionist's voice boomed, 'why do you wish to join my company, Mr *Irving*?'

Corbett hesitated, noticing how the illusionist laid heavy emphasis on the pseudonym, and he wondered if his cover had been compromised, but could think of no reason it should be. Before Corbett could answer, Lucifer replied to his own question.

'I suppose you – like everyone else – want to learn my secrets. Very well: you shall. But you cannot learn any of my secrets until you have been initiated. This will take place in three days' time, during your first performance, by which time you will – I hope – have learnt a few simple illusions. My disciples will look after you. Good morning.'

The illusionist waved his hand imperiously and Corbett was ushered out and taken to another studio. He was told by two of Lucifer's assistants to remove his jacket, tie and shirt. He did as he was asked and was given a white period shirt to wear. He was then photographed, full face and two profiles. They then measured him thoroughly and cut off a small lock of his hair.

'All part of the illusion?' Corbett enquired.

'For the costume fitting,' one of the assistants replied. 'Be here at ten tomorrow morning to attend the rehearsal. And don't be late.'

The assistants turned their backs on him dismissively, so he dressed hurriedly and left the building. As soon as he was out in the street he cursed himself for being such a fool. He had brought his wallet with him, which contained his identity, and he felt that while he was having his photograph taken, he may have been searched. He couldn't be certain. It was just one of his suspicious intuitions.

Feeling agitated, he strolled through the crowded streets and walked the five miles to his office, hoping the exercise might lessen the growing unease he felt about joining the Great Lucifer's organisation. But infiltrating the illusionist's company was the only way he could think of to investigate young Callas's disappearance.

Once he reached his office, the comfort of familiar territory, his tension faded, and he busied himself with recording visual messages for his website, apologizing for his absence from the office for at least a week, saying anyone who needed his services could contact him on his cell phone or leave a message. He thought of recording details of his whereabouts just to be on the safe side, then told himself he was being paranoid, and there really was nothing to worry about. He was certain the Great Lucifer was merely a showman, like one of those old-fashioned method actors who lived the part. And Corbett felt confident that once he was accepted in his company, he might break through the barrier, get to know the man, and question him about Robert Callas's disappearance.

***

On the first day of rehearsal at the illusionist's studio, Corbett was asked to sign a confidentiality declaration and made to hand over his cell phone, which would be returned to him once he was truly initiated into Lucifer's company. With some reluctance, he did as he was asked, wondering if he might find time during a break in rehearsals to purchase another.

'The Great Lucifer guards his secrets zealously,' he was told by one of the illusionist's acolytes. 'So please don't consider using another cell phone.'

Although Corbett felt exasperated by the demands they made, he did – however grudgingly – appreciate their need for secrecy. If they were about to reveal some of the illusionist's secrets, they wouldn't want him rushing out to phone any closely guarded secrets to another magician or the media. But what he learnt over the three-day rehearsal period was not exactly enthralling, and he gained no more arcane knowledge than he might have acquired from purchasing a child's box of conjuring tricks. And he didn't see anything of Lucifer except at the end of the third day, when the illusionist summoned him to the stage of the theatre and told him soon it would be time, and he had been chosen to understudy an important role.

'Which one is that?' he asked.

'One which will solve your problem,' was the enigmatic reply.

***

On the night of his debut Corbett took a stiff brandy to calm his nerves. He hadn't been on stage since he was a small boy and hadn't considered the possibility that he might suffer from stage fright. During the half hour wait before the show he puffed nervously on his e-cigarette. He was told to remain in his dressing room and under no circumstances was he allowed to wander round the theatre.

But when the show began, Corbett decided to risk a bit of a snoop around. He opened the dressing room door and stuck his head out, but there was one of the disciples, dressed as an executioner, standing guard at the end of the corridor.

'We'll call you when you're required,' he said.

Corbett stuck his head back in and shut the door. He paced nervously up and down, puffing vapour from his e-cigarette as he listened to the show relay system. Incantation followed incantation, followed by thunderous applause at the end of each trick. But for Corbett the time dragged. Would anything go wrong with his trick? he wondered. It seemed straightforward enough, disappearing through a trapdoor. But he was still no nearer to solving the mysterious disappearance of Robert Callas.

A burst of applause, then the babble of the audience, told him it must be the interval. He stuck his head outside the door again.

'Excuse me,' he said to the executioner. 'But I thought I was to appear in the first half.'

'I expect there's been a change in the running order,' the executioner mumbled through his black mask. 'Your time will come.'

Corbett tutted impatiently and slammed the dressing room door. He spent the next hour staring at his worried reflection in the mirror, unable to think clearly. Suddenly he started. He hadn't heard the executioner enter. The man smiled behind the mask which half covered his face.

'You are required to fulfil your obligation as an understudy,' he said.

'But I don't know which part I'm understudying.'

'Almost the star part. The climax of the evening.'

'N-not the man to be hanged,' Corbett stammered.

Seeing the detective falter, the executioner took him gently by the arm from the dressing room and guided him towards the stage. 'There is nothing to be afraid of. The illusion has always worked perfectly. I promise you.'

'I expect it's done with a harness,' Corbett said, more for his own benefit.

They arrived in the darkness backstage. A small blue light glowed, making everything seem strange and distorted. Corbett was ordered to place his hands behind his back, and someone tied them together.

'Not so tight,' the detective gasped.

'It won't be for long,' the executioner whispered.

From the stage the Great Lucifer made his announcement in preparation for the finale. The scene-change curtains rose swiftly, and lights burst in Corbett's face. The lights were too strong for him to see the audience, but he could feel their insatiable appetite for horror. He was pushed roughly by the executioner's assistant up the steps of the scaffold. As he reached the top, he became aware there was something missing from the scene. How had he missed that when he saw the show from the comfort of the dress circle? There was no priest. Why was there no priest?

He felt the noose being thrust over his head. It tightened, pinching his skin. He tried to tell them, but they were too immersed in their roles. And he wanted to ask them about the harness. Where was the harness? It was almost time and there was no harness.

The drum began to beat, and the executioner placed his hand on the lever. The audience was silent and still; nobody dared cough or move. He stared at Lucifer. Where *had* he seen that face before? In a book somewhere, or a painting? As he desperately tried to find an answer in the Great Lucifer's face, he became aware that he was being told something. Instinctively he obeyed the illusionist's tacit command and looked into the wings, hoping to discover the answer to the trick part of the illusion.

At first his mind was numbed by what he saw, staring at another actor standing next to a coffin. He couldn't quite comprehend what it was he was seeing. Then he reacted with horror when he realised this other actor standing in the wings was himself. The same hair, the same colour eyes, the same height, everything. And the actor looked up at Corbett and smiled. And Corbett knew why.

He began to scream with terror. Someone in the audience laughed. The drumbeat changed into a roll. His scream froze. He tried to tell the audience – to tell them what had happened to his client's son. It was too late. The drum

Dalek, about three inches tall, a plastic Tyrannosaurus Rex, a little silver pistol he had appropriated from a Monopoly game, his teddy bear and a small Batmobile. Beneath the Batmobile lay his Marvel comic, the one he always enjoyed reading, because he never remembered the plot, and so it was unfailingly a pleasant surprise to become acquainted yet again with some of the characters, many of whom were forgotten daily, but seemed like vaguely familiar friends. As he raised the Batmobile from the comic, an instinctive vroom sound-effect escaped from his throat. He was about to start reading when he was distracted for a moment by an echoing, spooky sound. Across the far side of the lounge, Mr Loman was making those funny noises that sounded like the courtship of whales. Frankie shook his head and smiled tolerantly. He didn't mind people who made strange noises. His eyes darted to the other side of the lounge where other residents sat in a semi-circle of chairs gazing mindlessly at a cooking programme on the television. The food appealed to Frankie, but he got bored with seeing how it was made and would have preferred to watch something with endless explosions, car chases and violence. Cooking was for wimps. Not for a tough guy like Frankie.

His lips moving silently as he began to read his comic, he was soon distracted when he heard a rustling sound beside him. It was Agnes, in her freshly-starched uniform. He gave her his usual lascivious grin. She returned his smile, her attractive face close to his, and he imagined her wearing a mink coat, bright-red lipstick and dangerously high heels as he swaggered, her arm through his, along a lengthy red carpet to collect a Hollywood Oscar for his gangster role, the one where he tortured the chief of police because the idiot wouldn't accept a bribe.

'Almost time for bed, Frankie,' Agnes said. 'I've just got to give Mr Loman his medication. Be right back.'

Frankie shrugged audacious shoulders in his leather jacket as he watched Agnes glide across the lounge towards the insufferable Loman, and called after her, 'Loman's a rat-faced fink. Slip him a Mickey Finn.'

He watched her movements for a moment, staring at her undulating backside before returning to his comic. He turned a page and read aloud, 'Say your prayers, Laser Man. You ain't got... got... Crack! Ker Pow! Was this the end of Laser Man?'

As the cartoon images danced in front of his eyes like familiar figures, his eyelids felt like something was weighing them down. Heavier and heavier. The colourful drawings of the page blurred, and he let his eyes close. Such a relief. Drifting into oblivion. But suddenly, a hand on his shoulder shook him awake. He opened his eyes. It was Agnes, her face large and threatening.

Her eyes colder than usual, she smiled slowly, and then her lips parted to reveal her brilliant white teeth, two long incisors, sharp and menacing, like a venomous snake about to poison him with its fangs. He shrunk back in his chair.

But Agnes seemed unconcerned. She reverted to her practical nurse temperament and consulted her wristwatch. 'Tainted blood!' she said. 'I'm late. I'm late. Must get a move on.' And then, in one fluid movement, she glided across the floor towards the door.

'Hey! Where you going?' Frankie called.

She turned around, smiled at Frankie, and gestured for him to follow. Dazed and obedient, his curiosity aroused to a feverish excitement, Frankie struggled out of his chair and hurried across the lounge. He was afraid of losing Agnes and missing an adventure of a lifetime. Although, from somewhere deep inside his head, a voice boomed an ominous warning, suggesting it might be more of an adventure of a deathtime. But what did that matter? After all, didn't Agnes look after him? Give him his Coco-Pops in the morning. Tuck him up at night.

Out in the hall, he caught the tail-end of Agnes disappearing into the broom cupboard. He had to hurry now or risk losing her. He dashed across the reception area and threw open the cupboard door. It was dark inside, but he was so involved in chasing after Agnes, he was unafraid. As he shut the door behind him, he expected the usual tangle of cleaning implements and was surprised to find the space empty, but a spectral light shone from somewhere, focused on a cupboard at chest height. On the cupboard was a picture of a Big Mac with the words EAT ME.

'Cor! Yummy!' he said as he licked his lips and pulled open the cupboard, hoping there were fries to go with the burger.

Then fear gripped him like a frozen hand around his throat, and the hairs on the back of his neck felt like needles of ice. Hanging in the cupboard was his teddy, a noose around the bear's neck. Someone – or something – had murdered his beloved Mr Teddy. He slammed the cupboard door shut as beads of sweat broke out under his arms, and he felt hot and cold shivers all over his body. Then the spectral light cut off his vision as the space was plunged once more into darkness. He froze. And then he felt something pass across his face, like a thin, slightly damp, ribbon. What was it? Ugh! It was a spider's web, and he hated and feared spiders. A fearful scream was blocked in his throat by what felt like a chunk of stone, and his body shook and shuddered as his brain seized up. Numb with terror, he knew the only option was to feel his way back along the wall to the entrance, so that he could return to the safety of the lounge, but he was frozen, too scared to do anything, in case he felt a spider. He imagined how big it was, with its huge hairy legs and bulbous eyes. He had to do something. Escape from the darkness. But where was the door?

Suddenly, an eerie creaking sound made him jump, and a door opened at the far end of the cupboard. Light flooded into the passageway as a hand appeared around the door frame, and long, painted fingernails like talons, slid around the door frame. The stone in Frankie's throat seemed to swell, and he had difficulty breathing. 'Mummy! he cried, as the hand was followed by a black and purple cloak. Sheathed inside the cloak was a Gorgon-like woman, the kind Frankie had only ever seen in a comic.

Although he was petrified, never having known such terror before, Frankie's mind still managed to register how attractive the woman was: her full lips, smooth skin, and wide blue eyes beneath feathery flaxen hair. And then she smiled, revealing sharp fangs as she hissed, moving closer to Frankie, her vampire teeth shining like deadly poisonous fangs.

'W-who are you?' Frankie stammered.

The vampire gave a small snake-like hiss before replying. 'I am Clarissa Cobra. Another bloodsucker.'

'Work for a city bank, do you?' Frankie chuckled nervously. Although he failed to grasp the meaning of his reply, he somehow thought it was a smart thing to say. And then he flinched as the vampire raised a hand to silence him.

'Silence! It is time you attended the coven dinner.'

'I'm feeling a bit peckish. You got any chips?'

Clarissa Cobra's body twisted enticingly, and her cavernous mouth opened invitingly as she stared at Frankie, her eyes gleaming like unnatural glass buttons. 'Oh yes, Frankie, we have plenty of chips for you?'

Frankie frowned deeply. 'How is it you know my name?'

'We know everything about you, Frankie. Everything! Now follow me.'

Clarissa beckoned Frankie to follow her, waving at him elegantly before exiting through the creaking door. Keen to distance himself from the spider-threatening environment, Frankie had no option other than to follow. He shuffled along the dark passageway towards the chink of light streaming through a gap in the door, his carpet slippers scuffing the rough surface. Pushing open the heavy door, he saw that it led into a dense thicket. He stepped forward cautiously, consoling himself that if the nightmarish garden proved to be too terrifying, he could always brave the broom cupboard and seek safety by returning to the residents' lounge. He was just about to turn around when there was an almighty bang, echoing in his head, like the slam of a coffin lid. It was the door leading back to the broom cupboard and the safety of the residents' lounge. He searched desperately for the door handle, but there wasn't one. The door was shut tight and there was no way of opening it. He was stuck here in this garden, surrounded by a thicket of thorny branches. All he could do now was to follow Clarissa through the gap in the thicket, but he remained immobile, his legs refusing to take orders from his brain. And then he remembered Clarissa had promised him chips to eat.

As he pictured a great big bowl of chips, life returned to his legs and spurred him on. He hurried through the gap in the thicket.

'Ouch!' he cried as a thorn scraped his hand. Elbowing his way through the thicket, he came to a gap on the other side and a wide path. He stopped and surveyed his surroundings. He was standing in a cemetery. Large gravestones dotted everywhere, like ghastly teeth, some covered in moss and lichen, some with coffin-like slabs of stone beneath them, and all the cemetery trees were ancient and rotting, gnarled with thick tendons of ivy curling around their trunks, and the trees cast threatening shadows everywhere, creating silhouettes of frightful figures. The gravestones appeared to go on for miles and the light was fading fast. Although there was still a little daylight left, the sky was overcast and sombre, a grey heavy blanket that covered the cemetery like a shroud.

Frankie walked cautiously along the path through the never-ending gravestones, muttering to himself as he went, 'Where am I? Oh help! I don't like this.'

A flap of wings startled him, and he ducked. What was it? A bat or a bird of some sort? And then a great squawk frightened him. It was a crow, perched on an enormous tombstone, high above, staring at him as he shuffled along. It was unnerving. The creature's eyes seemed to follow him, and it looked as if it might swoop down at any moment and peck him to death. Frankie shuddered and hurried along the path. Glancing back over his shoulder, he noticed the crow had gone, had vanished like a ghostly apparition. But ahead of him was another horrific creature, sitting on a gravestone. Normally, Frankie didn't mind cats, but this black cat was terrifying as it had only one eye, which stared with satanic satisfaction at the intruder, its only eye the personification of evil.

Relieved to see the path rounded a corner by a great oak tree, Frankie was glad to get out of sight of the evil-looking cat. As he turned the corner, he was surprised to see Clarissa talking to Agnes, and another woman and a man. Agnes was now dressed similarly to Clarissa, wearing a dark cloak with a hood, as was the other woman, and the man wore a white cotton jacket, the sort of coat a hospital orderly might wear. The group was perched on a tombstone, and the giant slab was laid for supper, with crockery, knives and forks, and bowls with lids on, containing what Frankie hoped would be chips – or at least food of some sort. But there was something vaguely unsettling about this group of weirdos, which struck Frankie as being reminiscent of a story his mother had once read to him.

One of the women, her jet-black fringe covering her eyes, pointed a painted fingernail at Frankie and peered at him as if she was examining a rather disgusting specimen in a Petri dish. 'Is this our new victim?' she asked. And then as Clarissa flashed her a warning sign, she corrected herself. 'Um – I mean, of course, our new recruit.'

'Who are you?' Frankie asked

'I am Vera Vomit. And this,' she added, pointing to the man, 'is Doctor Spritzer.'

Frankie nodded agreeably. 'Oh, I expect he makes you feel better.'

Agnes startled Frankie with her cackling laugh. 'He does that all right. Especially after Vera's had a night painting the town red.'

'Yes, blood red,' Vera screeched. The three vampires laughed hysterically, and their laughter reverberated in the cemetery like sound waves bouncing off tin walls, which left Frankie feeling confused but also reckless. Which was a good reason, he felt, for participating in the merriment.

'Ketchup's red, innit?' he guffawed like a lunatic to ingratiate himself with these misfits, hoping chips would soon be served.

Clarissa Cobra raised a hand. 'Silence!' she hissed, cutting through his laugh like a knife slicing an artery. 'It is time for your treat. Prepare to enjoy a wonderful initiation,'

'Does that go with chips?'

Agnes leaned forward and waved a bottle of ketchup in his face. 'No, but this does, Frankie.'

'Enjoy your food, Count Frankula,' Clarissa said, handing him a plate piled high with chips.

Frankie's jaw slackened, his eyes clouded over, and a gormless expression settled in his face. 'Count who? Who's that then?'

'That will be you. Very soon.'

Frankie grabbed the plate of chips, put it on the tombstone, took the cap off the ketchup bottle and poured. As they watched him smothering his chips with sauce, the three vampires exchanged looks and tittered.

'Soon you will be one of us,' Dr Spritzer said, and produced a cloak which he put over Frankie's shoulders.

An expert on junk food, Frankie regarded the ketchup suspiciously. 'Bit runny this sauce, if you ask me.' He raised the chip plate to his face and sniffed. 'Ugh! This ketchup don't smell right.'

Vera Vomit glared at him, her eyes piercing. 'Ketchup! What in Satan's name is ketchup? That's blood. Vampire blood.'

'B-b-b-blood,' Frankie stammered. 'I feel faint. I can't stand the sight of blood.'

'I will soon cure you,' Agnes said. 'And become the eater of your soul.'

'That's all right. I'm not one for fish. Prefer burgers, me.'

'Enough! It is time to draw blood.'

Frankie almost fainted, and his body shook with fear. 'Help! Mummy!' he cried and pulled the cloak over his head. In the blackness of the cloak he sought comfort, sheltering from the death-mask faces of the women, and the glassy expressionless stare of the weird doctor. He felt dizzy, his head swam in a whirlpool as he was pulled down into a vortex, swirling around and around, and a great gushing noise of a cataract deafened him, and the ringing in his ears pained him. Then, suddenly, everything stopped. As though time stood still. All was quiet, and he now felt soothed and relaxed, as though he was lying in his bed. But his bed was rock hard. He raised his head from beneath the cloak and found himself lying on a hard tombstone. Positioned one either side of him on adjoining graves were Agnes and Dr Spritzer. The doctor had a notebook in his hand, and his voice was soothingly precise as he talked to Agnes.

'Clearly he has an irrational fear of blood.' To Frankie, he said, 'When did you first fear blood? Can you remember?'

Frankie tilted his head back and looked up through the overhanging branches at the darkening sky as he tried to remember. 'Um – let me see. It must have been when I fell off me BMX.'

Puzzled, Spritzer looked to Agnes for guidance. She shrugged as she tried to work it out.

'B is for blood. And M is for mother, perhaps.'

'And the X?' the doctor demanded.

Agnes racked her brains for what could possibly have affected Frankie. The first two letters seemed to make perfect sense, but the third posed problems with the analysis. She heard Spritzer tutting impatiently, so she ventured a guess. 'Xylophone,' she offered weakly.

'Ridiculous!' Spritzer snapped.

'What else could it be?'

'No matter. We're wasting time. He must take the cure. Nurse – you know what you must do.'

Agnes leaned in close to Frankie, her lips hovering near his neck. 'How would you like to join us, Frankie?' she whispered seductively. 'And become one of the living dead.'

Frankie frowned. 'Would I have to sing? I'm not very good at singing.'

'All we need from you is your blood.'

She snarled, and a hiss escaped from her throat. When Frankie saw the teeth, like daggers of death, he panicked. 'Help! I wanna go home.'

As Agnes lunged at his neck, he raised the cloak to protect himself, then summoned strength he never knew he had in him to rise hurriedly from his position on the slab and run as fast as he could through the cemetery. But as he tore past an ornate marble sepulchre, from behind a pillar Clarissa Cobra, long talons like a bird of prey, reached for his throat. He dodged her clutches and changed direction, stumbling across tombstones, and tripping in overgrown weeds and brambles. One of his slippers came off, but he didn't dare stop to retrieve it because he thought he heard a panting noise behind. Then he stopped as Vera Vomit blocked his way. And from another direction he saw Agnes and Doctor Spritzer approaching. And the panting noise he heard from behind was Clarissa moving in for the kill. He was surrounded. There was no escape. In the distance, he could see a church spire, and the bells began ringing loudly, but the awful clanging sound seemed to be in his head, getting louder and louder. And then a spectral voice boomed, 'And as the village clock strikes three, will there still be blood for tea?' The vampires echoed, 'Blood! Blood! Blood! as they closed in on Frankie, who was almost bent double as he cowered and covered his ears to escape the cacophony of doom. 'Argh! Mummy! he screamed for his mother to rescue him from this nightmare.

'Wake up, Frankie! Agnes shook him by the shoulder.

Frankie's eyes blinked open, but he was still disorientated, and failed to notice the plate of chips in Agnes's hand. 'No, I'll be good,' he cried. 'I won't tell no more lies or threaten to burn Mummy's hair off – ever again.'

Agnes smiled knowingly. 'You must have dozed off. Had a bad dream, did you?'

Realising he was in the safe confines of the common room, Frankie smacked his right fist into his left palm, and his rubbery lips arranged themselves into a boastful image. 'Nothing F. A. couldn't handle. There ain't a monster in the world could scare the wits off of me.'

'Of course not, Frankie. Now here's your supper. Chips again. Your favourite.' Agnes placed the plate on the table beside his chair and showed him a bottle of ketchup. 'And I know how much you like your tomato sauce—'

'No! No! Take it away. It reminds me of blood. Bring me some brown sauce, instead.' He shivered, and shrank into the chair, shielding his face from the blood-red ketchup.'

'Don't be silly, Frankie,' Agnes began. 'You know you like—'

'I'm cold,' he complained, then looked down at his feet. 'No wonder. Something's happened to one of me slippers.'

Agnes laughed, and that was when Frankie looked up and saw a cruel glint in her eye, and an inhuman smile that revealed two sharp fangs.

'Slipper!' Agnes hissed. 'Let's wait until dark and return to the cemetery to look for it. And there's a full moon tonight. Just the night for a walk in the cemetery.'

'Mummy!' yelled Frankie.

3: Terra Incognita

The public house was situated halfway up the mountain and could only be reached by a winding road, too narrow for two cars to pass each other. There were a few passing points, but not enough, which meant a driver meeting another car head on might have to reverse as much as two or three hundred yards, hoping another car might not arrive behind and cause chaos. Which rarely happened, because very few people bothered to journey to the pub, and folks in the nearby town wondered how it managed to stay open. No food was served, and even at the height of summer visitors stayed for only one drink, glad to shake off the gloomy atmosphere of this unwelcoming pub.

The pub was appropriately named the Lamb, because sheep were the only hardy creatures that survived the bleak winters on this rugged peak. The pub was the highest building on the mountain, and the nearest farmsteads were at least three miles down from it, and as the town was only three miles away from the nearest farms, most of the farmers chose to drink in the town.

It wasn't a large town, with a population of only sixteen thousand. It had two hotels, with bars open to non-residents, three pubs, one of which had a restaurant annexe, and these establishments made enough money to survive the harsh winters from the influx of tourists descending on the town from early spring to mid-autumn. Out of season, the three pubs catered to just a few loyal regulars, and one of the pubs, the Eagle, was situated on a corner opposite the narrow mountain road leading to the six-mile drive to the Lamb. Every Saturday night, for the past three weeks since late October, customers in the Eagle glimpsed a minibus turning onto the mountain road. The vehicle, which was invariably full of people, gave rise to thunderous gossip. Who were these strangers attracted to the funereal ambience of the Lamb? Where were they from? They weren't locals. Yet every Saturday night at around seven p.m., locals at the Eagle stared out of the pub's windows as the minibus turned onto the mountain road and began its long ascent to the most unpopular pub in the county.

Of course, being a small town, the gossip was not confined to the Eagle, and spread throughout the district. During the summer, because the town was so busy, the Lamb was rarely mentioned, except when hikers and climbers made an unplanned visit to its dingy bar and were served by a landlord who clearly hated customers. Locals told visitors that it was entirely on their own heads; they couldn't deny they hadn't been warned about visiting the Lamb.

On the third Saturday of the dreary November evening following the minibus's sudden appearance, a regular in the Eagle spotted it turning onto the mountain road for its fourth visit to the Lamb. Now the idle hands of winter jumped on juicy gossip about the mysterious strangers who travelled to their small town to drink at not only the worst pub in the county, probably the worst in the country.

It being almost winter, and the Eagle regarded as the most old-fashioned, though rather traditional, of the town's three pubs, there were only five regulars and one newcomer present, all sitting at the bar on stools. Derek, a retired man with a wizened face, who spotted the minibus, spoke as if he knew something none of the others in the bar did.

'That minibus is full of surveyors. Definitely surveyors going up there.'

The landlord, Tim, a heavy, beef-red man in his fifties, frowned at Derek. 'How d'you work that out?'

'Stands to reason. Regular visits. Probably planning to rebuild the Lamb. Big hotel, maybe.'

A local farmer, Glyn, snorted into his beer. 'Don't talk daft. Who'd want to spend a fortune on building a hotel up there? The Lamb's too small to expand and there's not enough car parking space for a hotel.'

Others nodded their heads in agreement. No one argued with Glyn, a broad-shouldered man with enormous, spade-like, calloused hands.

'And the access is bloody terrible,' another regular opined.

The pub landlady, Dilys, the only woman in the bar, sat on a stool near the counter flap. 'I'll tell you what's really weird,' she said, grabbing everyone's attention. 'Last Saturday night I couldn't get to sleep, so I got up to make myself a cuppa. Three in the morning it was. I heard this car, so I looked out the window. And there was that minibus that went up to the Lamb just after seven coming back.'

'What's weird about that?' Derek wanted to know.

Tim answered for his wife. 'I'll tell you what's weird, what don't make sense. Nobody goes up to that pub at night. God knows how it manages to stay open. And then suddenly, out of the blue, they have customers in a minibus like they're on some sort of outing. Total strangers, who come back long after closing time.'

'Aye, but it's not like the law's going to do them for after-hours drinking,' Derek argued. 'Not up there.'

Glyn laughed ironically. 'I think what Tim means is, it's weird how strangers – a whole party of 'em – shoot through the town and go up to the Lamb for a night out. Not the best place to go drinking, as we know.'

Glyn's friend, John, a small wiry man, banged his glass on the bar and said, 'I went there once, and that was enough. He hasn't even got proper beer pumps. Just barrels behind the bar. The only time I was there, I had a pint, and it tasted like gnat's piss. That licensee should be chucked out.'

Tim shook his head. 'Free house, ain't it? Not tied to any brewery.'

A balding man in his late forties, sitting at the far end of the bar, a little apart from the other drinkers, looked up from his newspaper and said, 'Anyone know much about the history of the Lamb? Why it was built halfway up the mountain.'

'And,' Glyn emphasised, 'whoever built it must have built the road leading to it as well. Because the road only leads to the pub.'

A silence followed. No one wanted to admit knowing nothing about its history, never having given it much consideration in the past, other than indulging in rumours about the current landlord.

'My name's Clive Brakway,' the man added. 'I'm new to the area, having lived here less than a month. And from the stories I heard about the pub, I decided I'd look it up in the library. The little library in town had no information on it. So, I tried the county library next time I was over there. Same thing. Hit a brick wall. Well, almost. I did discover the pub was built in 1902, in front of caves which apparently go back quite a way, deep into the mountain.'

'That would save building a beer cellar,' Derek said. 'The caves at the back would be a useful storage space. Who built the pub? Did you find out?'

'A man by the name of Digby Carnivean. It didn't say much about him. Just his birth and death. He died in 1949. Anyone know what the current licensee's name is?'

'Carnivean,' Tim answered. 'Initial J.'

'So he could be the son or grandson.'

'Judging by the landlord's age – he looks to be in his fifties. Hard to tell really. But I'd guess it's the grandson.'

'I wonder what he does up there all by himself if he never has customers?'

'Except on a Saturday when he gets these strange visits,' Derek corrected him.

'He must come down to the town for supplies sometimes. I know the pub doesn't do food, but he must need stuff for himself.'

Dilys smacked her hands together and smiled. 'I can put you in the picture there. Sharon at the checkout in the supermarket says he comes in every Friday at ten, regular as clockwork, and buys up the shop. Much more stuff than for one person.'

'But if he don't do food at the pub—' Derek commented.

'But the bulk buying's only been going on for the past three weeks,' Dilys cut in.

Glyn smiled and shook his head. 'It looks as if Mr-whatever-his-initial-stands-for Carnivean is getting supplies for the Saturday night minibus crowd.'

Everyone in the bar was quiet for a moment while they thought about this. John, Glyn's mate, was the first to break the silence.

'Very strange,' he said, looking at his watch. 'Maybe we should take a drive up there and check it out.'

Glyn shook his head. 'Six miles there, and six miles back, along that narrow road in the dark. Waste of valuable drinking time. Maybe another Saturday.'

Mutterings in the bar as other customers concurred, especially the landlord, who could see the revenue of his two regulars diminishing.

Clive Brakway swallowed the last of his pint and placed the empty glass on the bar.

Tim walked over to him. 'Another?'

'No, just the one tonight. I'll catch you another night.'

He left the pub hurriedly, knowing the gossip might now be directed at himself, the newcomer and stranger in town. He strolled back through the almost deserted streets towards his hotel, hoping nobody in the bar discovered he was staying there, because he was only in the town temporarily to investigate the mystery of the Lamb.

***

Sitting at the small unit in his hotel room, Brakway opened his laptop and studied his notes on the Lamb. He hoped he wasn't wasting his time and the mystery of the pub turned out to be nothing more than... what? A useless landlord unable to cope with running an out-of-the-way pub? The mountain was situated in an area of natural beauty, and anyone with half an ounce of common sense would realise there could be a reasonably good summer trade running a pub that served good food.

No, there had to be something more to the run-down pub than ineffectual management.

The more Brakway thought about it, the more the Lamb looked like a contender for a good story. And he needed that scoop. By Christ did he need it. Redundant after nearly twenty years loyal service to his newspaper, and then the cutbacks and downsizing. Becoming a freelance. Meaning he had to source his own stories. Then the problems of funding his own research. Expenses eating up his savings.

Like the hotel. Not cheap, even though it was well out of season.

He stared at the laptop screen, reading his notes on the story. What story? Was he kidding himself?

It began just over a month ago. Eavesdropping on a furtive meeting in a London gastro pub, he picked up snippets of a whispered conversation. And he thought he recognised one of the men, a familiar face he couldn't quite place. The huddled group consisted of three men and two women, and he was intrigued by their conspiratorial behaviour; a guilty glance over the shoulder if one of them let slip a word too loudly. He sat very close to them, doing what he often did when picking up information. Buried his head in a newspaper and listened intently.

After the group split up, he followed the man he thought he recognised out of the pub and along Knightsbridge. The man, probably in his early sixties with longish white hair, wearing an immaculate finely-tailored two-piece suit, disappeared into Harrods. In the menswear department, the man purchased a flamboyant silk scarf. And it was this sartorial trademark which helped him to identify the man. Recognition came to him in a flash. It was Lord Pelhambury. He recognised him from his occasional appearances on the television news.

As Brakway stared at his laptop screen, searching for clues, he sensed he wasn't mistaken in his ability to sniff out a sensational story. Why, he asked himself, would a peer of the realm, and others whom he had been unable to identify, drive every Saturday night for the past four weeks, nearly two hundred miles to a squalid, run-down pub halfway up a mountain? The enigma was sinister, intriguing and compulsive.

And it could be a story every freelance journalist could only dream about, he decided.

The trouble was, he was stuck in the hotel room, and investigating the minibus's arrival at the Lamb was six nights away. And he didn't think the Eagle could offer any more than the scant information he'd heard tonight.

On the other hand, it was Sunday tomorrow, and the weather forecast was good. Don't many people go out for a drink Sunday lunchtime? It wouldn't look suspicious if he turned up at the Lamb around one p.m., and if the landlord questioned him, he could say he had just moved to the area and was getting to know the district. It would at least give him a feel for what to expect next Saturday.

Confident, and excited by the prospect of an important story, he shut down his laptop and stared at his reflection in the unit's mirror. What stared back at him was his boyish, earnest expression. He had worn well over the years, despite the heavy drinking as he faced cold redundancy. His face, roundish with not many wrinkles, revealed not a hint of stress from his job, the boozing, or the divorce from his wife who gained custody of their only daughter.

He sighed deeply, bored, knowing he had much time to kill during this investigation. The unearthing of a sensational story could sometimes prove tedious in its early stages.

He stared at the television set, scowled at it, knowing Saturday was the worst night of the week for showing reality celebrity rubbish. Maybe there was a film he could watch starting much later. But it was only just gone eight o'clock, so there would be a gap of two or three hours to kill until the late-night film. He had drunk only one pint of lager in the Eagle, so if he stuck to just one more pint, and two whisky chasers in the hotel bar, he reckoned the alcohol would have left his blood by Sunday lunchtime. There was no way he could risk another drink-driving offence, like the three-year ban almost a decade ago, which put pressure on both his job and marriage.

He took his laptop into the bar and ordered a pint of lager. There was only one other customer in the bar, who was about to speak to Brakway, but to avoid conversation Brakway turned away rudely and sat in a corner well away from him. He opened his laptop and began to study for the umpteenth time his notes on Lord Pelhambury, even though he didn't think he would learn anything he didn't already know. A privileged upbringing, and a degree in economics, Pelhambury went on to became a successful city trader, and many years later an arms manufacturer and dealer.

From what little he had seen of Lord Pelhambury in the media, the man oozed public charm. But as far as Brakway was concerned, the man was not to be trusted, with those over-sincere, glistening eyes.

***

Brakway wondered if regulars in the bar of the Eagle watched as he drove onto the mountain road leading to the Lamb. He smiled as he imagined the gossip his excursion generated as his Renault turned the corner.

The road was steep in places, winding through narrow spaces between large rocks. Sheep were scattered about the hillside like ornaments, turning their worried heads as the car climbed the steep gradients in low gear.

The six-mile journey was so circuitous it took him almost ten minutes. He spotted the building above him as the road, which was little more than a track, became less steep. He yanked the steering wheel round hard, taking the car sharply round a hairpin bend for the last hundred yards to the Lamb. The pub was set way back from the road, on a natural plateau, which made a perfect car park in front of and to the side of the pub. He saw one other car there, a large Volvo estate, and he wondered if this belonged to the landlord.

The pub was brick-built, with small leaded windows, the panes of glass coated in years of grime. The building was neglected and had he not known it was still open for business, albeit not a thriving one, he would have assumed it was derelict. Moss and weeds grew up from the muddy ground at the bottom of the building, tiles in the slate roof looked dangerously loose, and the chimney pot hung at a precarious angle, cracked in the middle, as if it had been struck by lightning. The building looked as if it should be condemned, and he wondered again about the mystery surrounding the Saturday night visitors.

He parked his Renault close to the landlord's Volvo and peered inside as he got out. But, other than a strange-looking hood, a sort of cowl, there was nothing else of interest. His feet crunched on gravel in front of the pub as he approached the scuffed oak door. It was opened by a latch above a large keyhole which he clicked down, not really expecting it to open. As it yawned open, creaking on its hinges, he was greeted by a stale smell, a vinegary sour taste in the back of his throat. He closed the door, and surveyed the empty bar, which with a little care and attention could have looked attractive. The low ceiling was oak beamed, and there was a large open fireplace, with a slate mantelpiece, on which stood two cracked toby jugs, and a battered tin ashtray with faded lettering on it which read Craven A. On one side of the fireplace was a highbacked settle, the seat covering frayed. On the other side of the fireplace was a large basket containing just three logs. There was a mound of ash in the fireplace, so it looked as if there had been a fire burning there recently. But for this time of the year it needed a fire burning constantly. The room felt cold and damp. Brakway shivered, wondering how anyone could face drinking in this uninviting atmosphere.

He walked up to the bar, coughed loudly, hoping to attract the landlord's attention. There was a sliding door behind the bar, sandwiched between two shelves with beer bottles, and beneath the shelves was one beer barrel and one cider barrel. There were no beer pumps on the bar. Above the shelves was a miserable selection of spirits on optics. He banged the counter loudly and called out:

'Hello?'

Suddenly, the sliding door rattled open on its runners, and Brakway found himself staring into the face of the landlord. He got the impression that the man had heard him arriving a little while ago but deliberately let him find the pub empty. Was it done to make him feel uneasy? Well, there was no way that was going to happen. He'd been in far worse situations during his journalistic career.

The landlord stared at him coldly, eyes as lifeless as glass marbles. A tough-looking man, over six feet tall, with a goatee beard and trim moustache. His sinewy frame looked like that of an acrobat, and it was difficult to tell his age. He could have been anywhere between forty and sixty.

'Mr Carnivean?' Brakway asked.

The landlord frowned deeply. 'Do I know you?'

Brakway shook his head and produced a pleasant smile. 'We've never met before. But if you're the licensee, your name is over the door.'

The landlord slid the door closed, and leaned on the bar counter, staring confrontationally at Brakway. 'Yes, I happen to be the licensee and landlord of this establishment. For my sins. What can I do for you?'

'A single measure of brandy please, Mr Carnivean.'

The landlord stared at him, almost as if it was an insult rather than a request for a drink. The two locked eyes for a moment, before Carnivean reached to a shelf above the bar to get a brandy glass, then turned to the optics.

'Bit quiet, isn't it?' Brakway observed cheerfully. 'Don't suppose you get much passing trade here.'

Carnivean banged the glass on the counter. 'That'll be four pounds.'

Brakway whistled astonishment as he took a five-pound note from his wallet. 'No wonder you're quiet. Single brandy down in the town's only three quid.'

Carnivean shrugged, his body language contemptuous as he grabbed Brakway's five-pounds and slammed a pound coin on the bar.

Brakway sipped the brandy and pocketed his change. Carnivean stared at him, arms wide, leaning on the counter. It seemed like a pose. Deliberately hostile and challenging. Determined he wasn't going to be intimidated, Brakway smiled nonchalantly.

'I was drinking in the Eagle last night,' he said. As the landlord showed no sign of responding, he added, 'And some of the regulars said they've seen a minibus coming up here every Saturday for the past month. I suppose private functions help when business is quiet in the winter months.'

Carnivean glared at him. 'Live in the town, do you?'

'Just moved here. That's why I thought I'd try all the local pubs. See where I might become a regular. I often like to sit quietly with a pint and read the paper.'

'I don't think you'll find anywhere quieter than the Lamb.'

'Except perhaps on Saturdays. When you have your minibus visitors.'

Carnivean tugged his goatee and stared fiercely at Brakway without replying.

Tilting his head at the fireplace, Brakway said, 'It must get very cold up here with no fire going.'

'I'm lucky. I don't feel the cold.'

'What about your Saturday guests, surely they must—'

'They'll be provided for,' Carnivean snapped. 'I'll be getting more logs the end of the week.' His eyes narrowed with suspicion as he studied Brakway. 'D'you work in the town?'

Brakway shook his head, his turn to play at Carnivean's game of silence, for which he took childish delight in this game of tit-for-tat.

'What is it you do for a living?'

Brakway looked at his watch, deliberately ignoring the landlord's question. 'Is that the time?' He swallowed the rest of his brandy. 'I must away. Just thought I'd acquaint myself with the nearest country pub. Uniquely situated halfway up a mountain. Be seeing you.'

As he walked towards the door, he felt an intense burning sensation in the back of his neck. He ignored it, presuming his imagination was triggered by the gloomy atmosphere of the pub and the landlord's inhospitable attitude.

He didn't look back, shut the door, and walked assuredly to his car. As he started the engine, he permitted himself a triumphant smile. Having known what to expect from the rude landlord hadn't fazed him.

As he drove back down the precipitous road, he thought again about Lord Pelhambury, wondering what an arms dealer would be doing visiting a grotty pub almost two hundred miles from London.

***

He glimpsed the checkout cashier's name badge as he entered the store. Sharon, a middle-aged woman with short, dark brown hair. He carried his basket to the wines and spirits section, selected a bottle of Courvoisier, then decided it was too expensive and replaced it with a bottle of Spanish brandy. He then got a selection of crisps and assorted nuts before returning to the checkouts. As it was early on a Monday morning, the store wasn't busy, and

Brakway lurked around the salad section until he saw Sharon was completely free.

As she swiped his items, he said, 'Went up to that strange pub yesterday, the Lamb. Up on the Mountain. I don't think I'll be going there again.'

She smiled and shrugged. 'Never been myself. But I've heard it's awful. Why anyone would want to go there—'

'And I asked the landlord if they did food. Nothing.'

'That *is* surprising. Cos he comes in here every Friday. Buys tons of grub. Can't be just for himself.'

'His shopping must take up a fair bit of time then.'

'I suppose about forty-five minutes. Then he goes and buys his logs.'

'Where does he get those from?'

She swiped the bar code on the last item from his basket. 'That'll be twelve pounds sixty.' As he took out his wallet, she pointed towards the store's automatic doors. 'Yeah, he asked about logs first time he came in here and I told him where he could get some. Five miles out of town that way, towards Bankstead.'

'How long would it take me, roughly, if I went over there?'

'To the log place? Oh, about ten minutes each way.'

He took his change, thanked her, and headed back to his hotel. Apart from guzzling brandy in his room, he wondered how he was going to kill time for the rest of the week. But at least he didn't have to wait until Saturday now. The landlord's shopping expedition, and the purchase of the logs would give him just over an hour to do some serious snooping on Friday morning.

He spent much of the rest of the week tearing his hair out as he searched the internet for details of the Carnivean family. The man who had the Lamb built, and the road leading to it, Carnivean's assumed grandfather, never married and had no children. There was not even a record of Carnivean's parents. Unless he was the progeny of an illegitimate child of Digby Carnivean. But there was no record of an illegitimate son. Nothing. Who then was Carnivean the landlord? Where did he come from, and why did he have the same surname as the man Brakway had assumed was his grandfather? And why couldn't he discover anything about the man? Nothing on social media. Nothing anywhere. No records of the man existed. He trawled through so many websites, including Births, Deaths and Marriages. Although he did find a website that gave minimal details of public houses in the area and discovered that the licensee's first name was Jack. Apart from that flimsy information, he drew a blank.

On Thursday night he was meticulous about his alcohol consumption, drinking no more than two pints of lager, and on Friday morning he drove to a street Carnivean would be sure to drive along to get from the mountain road to the supermarket. Because the landlord knew what sort of car Brakway drove, he made certain it was parked unobtrusively in an alley. A few minutes before ten o'clock he spotted Carnivean in his Volvo, heading in the direction of the supermarket. As soon as the man was out of sight, he pulled out of the alley and headed for the Lamb.

As it was drizzling, a fine rain made the going tougher on the drive up to the Lamb. It took him twelve minutes to reach the plateau. To avoid meeting the landlord on his return journey, he estimated he would have a clear forty minutes to investigate the pub. But if there was no way of gaining entry, he wouldn't need that long to nose around.

First, he tried the main entrance, which of course was locked. He put his face close to the windows and peered inside, but he saw nothing unusual in the gloom of the bar. He walked backwards and looked up, feeling the rain on his face. There were two upstairs windows and he guessed that those rooms were probably the landlord's living area, a bedroom and living room, maybe. There were no curtains on the windows, but who needed curtains in this remote area? He decided it was time to explore the side of the pub. To the left of the building toward the rear was another door beyond another poky window, also as grubby as the windows at the front. He pushed his face against one of the panes, cupping his eyes with his hands. All he could see was a kitchen sink, and beside it an electric cooker. He guessed there was no gas up here so presumably Digby Carnivean, or his successor, must have arranged for electricity to reach the Lamb. Next, he tried the door, which was also locked. Had it been a Yale type of key he might have tried to pick it, but the lock was the same as the main entrance. An accomplished housebreaker would have little difficulty gaining an entrance, but to an amateur like himself, the pub remained impenetrable.

He stepped back from the door to see if there was any way he might perhaps climb over it. But the pub was built into the side of the overhang of the mountain, with the door under part of the first floor of the pub. And then he noticed a small metal ornament, a disc built into the door at the top. And inside the circle of the disc was a grotesque gargoyle face. He stared at the face. There was something about one of the eyes.

Shit!

One of the gargoyle's eye sockets contained the dark glimmer of a CCTV camera lens. He'd been rumbled. He wondered if Carnivean had some sort of link to the CCTV and was watching him on a remote electronic device. Or was his snooping just being recorded inside the pub?

All he could do now was try damage limitation. Pretend he was simply being nosy. He knocked the door loudly, calling out 'hello' several times. He doubted it could be heard, but at least it might look as if he was trying to summon the landlord to answer. He shook his head, as if giving up on his attempts to get someone's attention, and then returned to his car.

That was when he suffered the second shock of his foolhardy exploit. His offside front tyre was flat, the wheel rim almost touching the ground. He looked at his watch. On top of the twelve-minute drive, and thinking he had plenty of time, he hadn't hurried as he casually investigated the pub, and had used up another ten minutes. He had no more than twenty minutes left – ten minutes to change the wheel, and ten minutes to drive back to the town.

He raised the boot and heaved the spare wheel out, along with the tools – a jack, tyre lever and wheel brace. Although it was cold and damp, he was starting to sweat. After he got the hub cap off, he slotted the brace on to one of the nuts and applied pressure. It wouldn't budge. He hadn't enough strength. He felt the veins bulging in his forehead as he tugged the brace with all his might, and still it wouldn't move. He sprayed the nut with WD40, then tried again, putting his back and body weight into it. He became angry, swearing at it. And then he felt it loosen and turn. Maybe the other nuts wouldn't be as difficult. But they were. By the time he had loosened them all, rivulets of sweat ran from under his arms. But at least now he could get the wheel off. He checked his watch. *Jesus!* This operation had so far cost him eight minutes. Now he only had twelve minutes left to jack up the car, change the wheel, tighten the spare, and return to the town. But by the time he had the wheel changed and tightened, and the tools put back in the boot, he saw he had only four minutes left to get down the mountain.

There was no way he could do it. His only hope was that Carnivean might have been held up. He sped down the narrow road, his offside wheels passing dangerously close to the edge, and the windscreen wipers pounding to and fro. The interior of the car misted up as his body heat generated condensation, so that it became difficult to see the curve of the road. And then he suddenly thought of a perfectly good excuse to visit the pub. Even if he'd been observed on the CCTV snooping around the back of the pub and staring through the window, he was certain his explanation would be satisfactory. He slowed down, continued along the road for another hundred yards, then pulled in at a passing space and waited. He had been there only five minutes, with the hot air blowing on full to clear his windscreen, when he spotted Carnivean's Volvo on the road just below.

The Volvo turned a hairpin and came up the narrow road towards his Renault. It stopped alongside, and Carnivean lowered his window, as did Brakway.

'What the hell d'you think you're doing?' Carnivean demanded. 'You must know pubs never open before noon. Don't try to kid me you came up here for a mountain walk.'

Brakway laughed. 'Of course not. I was hoping to talk to you.'

'What about?'

'Your pub's not tied to a brewery.'

'It's a free house. Belongs to me. So what?'

'It seems a shame it's so run down.'

'Is that any of your concern?'

'I suppose not. But I'm looking to buy a small business. And the Lamb could do a good food trade in the summer—'

'It's not for sale.'

'Yes, but—'

Brakway didn't get a chance to finish. Carnivean closed the window and drove off. Brakway chuckled. It had worked. Why hadn't he thought of that excuse earlier? It would have saved him panicking. Still, at least now he could return on Saturday in the role of a persistent purchaser, even though he'd been told it wasn't for sale.

***

As he walked into the Lamb on Saturday night at just gone eight, expecting to find a crowd of at least a dozen people, he was surprised to see only the landlord behind the bar, and Lord Pelhambury, sitting at a table opposite a blonde woman in her early forties, whom he recognised as the peer's wife. The minibus was parked outside, and customers in the Eagle had spoken about a crowd of people visiting the Lamb, so why were there only two of them? Surely Pelhambury hadn't driven the minibus up here himself. Where were the other customers?

Trying to mask the look of surprise on his face while listening intently for sounds of other people, Brakway was momentarily alarmed by the strange atmosphere into which he'd been drawn, almost as if they expected him. At least the pub was now marginally less uninviting as there was a blazing log fire in the grate.

'Good evening,' Lord Pelhambury said, the vowels of his greeting elongated like a poet's, but with sinister undertones. 'What brings you halfway up this mountain on such a misty night?'

'I might well ask you the same question.' Brakway replied. 'But haven't I seen you somewhere before?'

Pelhambury chuckled. 'Let's get the introductions over and done with, shall we? I'm Lord Pelhambury – but please call me Gordon. And this is my wife, Lady Pelhambury.'

'And you may call me Ursula,' Lady Pelhambury said. She looked up at Brakway with a smile that lacked warmth. 'And you are?'

'Clive Brakway.'

'Won't you join us, Clive?' her husband said with fake cordiality. 'And it's my round. What will it be?'

'Well, I hardly think—'

'Nonsense. Please be seated. And mine host will bring you whatever your poison is.'

As he sat down next to Lady Pelhambury, Brakway thanked him, and asked for a brandy. Pelhambury looked towards the landlord and demanded a large brandy.

'A small one will be fine,' Brakway protested. 'I have to drive.'

Pelhambury waved the objection aside. 'No coppers up in these parts, dear boy. Bring him a large one, Carnivean.'

'Thank you. You're most kind.'

'You're welcome. Our landlord tells me you were looking to buy this pub.'

Brakway nodded. 'That's right. I just thought perhaps in the summer—'

'However, I don't think the pub is up for sale. Isn't that right, Carnivean?'

As the landlord brought over the brandy, he almost snarled at Brakway. 'I told you on Monday it wasn't for sale.' He slammed the brandy onto the table. 'So why have you come back?'

Brakway ignored him and toasted Pelhambury. 'Thank you, Gordon. Cheers!'

'You're most welcome.'

Brakway took a large gulp of his drink, glad now that Pelhambury had ordered a double.

'You said you recognised me,' Pelhambury said. 'Where from, if you don't mind my asking?'

'It was on *Newsnight*. You were defending your stance on supplying arms to certain war- torn countries, and to regimes of which the British Government doesn't necessarily approve.'

'They turn a blind eye, dear boy. And it's worth billions in exports. Bottom line: that's all they care about.'

'And do you sleep well at night?'

'Nothing bothers me. To resort to a well-worn cliché, it's not guns that kill people, it's people that kill people.'

'But if it wasn't for the suppliers of those weapons—'

Pelhambury shrugged. 'And what about you?'

'Me? What about me?'

Brakway was aware the landlord, who hadn't moved since bringing the brandy, still stood close to his chair, invading his space. He knocked back the remainder of the brandy, intending to get up to go to the bar. But he stopped as Pelhambury leant forward, pointing an accusing figure at him.

'Yes, you Mr Brakway, searching for a sleazy story. Anything that sells papers.'

'How did you know I was a journalist?'

'Don't you mean hack? Oh, it wasn't difficult to get your name from the hotel you're staying at. And then the social media.'

Brakway suddenly felt vulnerable and tried to get up. But his legs felt weak, and his brain spun with spirals of monstrous images. He tried to speak but his voice was a distant echo. 'What about... what about these others? The minibus with... people.' His voice sounded slurred, his lips turned to rubber. What was it? Was it the brandy? He couldn't remember... anything. He heard laughter, macabre noises as faces opposite zoomed in and out of focus. Strange and deformed images swirled around in his head, spinning out of control, while a discordant high-pitched buzzing was frighteningly head-splitting. Distorted faces clamped revolting jaws over his head, swallowing him and screaming in his brain. He closed his eyes, glad to surrender the struggle, and fall into a black pit. Anything to shut out the hallucinations.

***

He heard chanting in the distance, as though it was part of his nightmare. Gradually he realised the chanting was very close. His mouth felt dry and his body ached. He tried opening his eyes, blinking rapidly. His arms ached, and he realised they were bound together by a rope. He was lying on the floor of a cavern, surrounded by figures in long robes, candlelight throwing flickering shadows across the cave walls.

'Beelzebub! Beelzebub! We offer this virgin sacrifice to you our most powerful leader,' a voice intoned.

He managed to sit up. His feet were also bound, tethered to a ring in the wall of the cave. He blinked again, forcing water into his eyes so that he could see clearer in the gloom. And then he was horrified by what he saw. Figures, cloaked in long flimsy robes with hoods, some male, some female, shuffled around a pentagram painted on the floor of the cave. All carried black candles in long wrought-iron holders, and a large, inverted crucifix hung upside down on one of the walls. A black chalice was passed around from which the group drank, and Carnivean, now wearing black robes, intoned, 'Drink, my perverted flock, from the blood of an innocent baby. This one no more than six months old.'

But what horrified Brakway more than anything and paralysed his blood with a terrifying fear of where the ceremony was leading was the altar on which lay a naked young girl, who couldn't have been more than ten-years-old, her legs and arms spread-eagled, bound by ropes at each wrist and ankle. A lethal-looking knife lay beside her.

'No!' he screamed. 'No! You can't do this.'

'Ah!' Pelhambury exclaimed. 'He's surfaced at last.'

He stood next to Carnivean, poised over the naked girl on the sacrificial altar. The landlord picked up the knife and handed it to Pelhambury. 'First you must kill the journalist.'

Pelhambury walked towards Brakway, while the other participants of this evil ritual gazed with fascination at what was about to happen, the dark shadows of their faces beneath their hoods looked like macabre graven images.

Brakway shrank into the rock wall, cowering as Pelhambury leant over him, the blade of the knife glinting as the peer gripped the handle tightly. Brakway, his head pressed hard against the wall, felt the steel against his throat and knew there was no escape from the inevitability of his death.

'Kill him, Gordon! Kill him!' chanted the peer's wife.

Brakway heard Pelhambury's intake of breath as the peer prepared to slit his throat. He closed his eyes, unable to imagine the pain and fear of death.

'Stop!'

It was Carnivean. His hand was raised imperiously.

'His death is not inevitable. He has a choice. He must commit his soul to Satan – the powerful one – if he wishes to continue to live in this life. Do you wish to live in this life, Brakway?'

Brakway, who didn't believe these people held any supernatural powers, and were merely a bunch of dangerous lunatics, knew that if he played along with the selling of his soul to escape death, then he might be able to persuade them – stop them – from killing the young girl.

'Yes,' he gasped. 'I'll do anything you ask. Sell my soul. Just as long as you let me live.'

Carnivean laughed humourlessly. 'You would say that, wouldn't you? Anything to escape death in this life. But to be accepted you must commit yourself to carry out the one act that brings you closer to him. You must sacrifice the girl.'

Tears sprang into Brakway's eyes, knowing there was no escaping this evil act. Lord Pelhambury, his mouth close to Brakway's ear, whispered, 'You won't just escape death by committing this act. You will have success in this life. Money, fame, luxury. You will never want for anything ever again. I can use this knife to free you, but you must promise to kill the girl. She may die in this life, but Carnivean will be giving her an immortality that few of us can imagine. Just say the one word and we will free you.'

Brakway's throat felt dry. 'Yes,' he whispered.

'What was that?' Carnivean demanded. 'Louder! We didn't hear you.'

'Yes! Yes! Yes!' Brakway yelled. 'I'll do it.'

Lord Pelhambury sniggered. 'And don't think about using the knife I give you on anyone else here. It can only be used on the sacrificial girl. Ursula is trained in combat.'

From a table behind the altar, Pelhambury's wife picked up a Roman short sword. Its blade glinted, and Brakway guessed that it was honed to a razor sharpness.

'Don't even think about attempting to use this knife I'm going to use to cut your ropes on anyone other than the girl. Is that understood?'

'Yes, I understand,' Brakway said, his mind racing as he tried to think of a way out of this terrible predicament.

And, as Brakway suspected, Ursula Pelhambury confirmed his worst fears. 'This sword is as sharp as a cut-throat razor. And believe me, I know how to use it.'

Lord Pelhambury cut the ropes that bound Brakway. He was helped to his feet by the peer and pulled over to the altar. His wife held her sword tightly, and Brakway felt she would relish an excuse to slash it across his throat. All it would take to kill him would be one fatal slash, or even a thrust into the breast which would go straight to the heart.

He was handed the knife from Pelhambury who took several steps back. He looked down at the helpless girl on the altar and saw her lips move. He bent over her, his ear close to her mouth.

'I'm not afraid,' she whispered. 'I will join him in another life.'

Brakway straightened up, as if he'd been shocked by an electric current.

'She is aware of her fate,' Carnivean said. 'It is written in her stars. Now it is time to commence with the sacrifice. Raise the knife high, bring it down hard with both hands, and plunge it deep into her breast,' he instructed Brakway.

Hands shaking, Brakway stood over the girl and raised the knife, tears now streaming down his face. The dark disciples of this black sacrifice began chanting, words that seemed meaningless to Brakway, as if they spoke in tongues. Their black candles flickered in the ghostly atmosphere.

'Do it!' Carnivean commanded.

'I can't,' Brakway said.

'What?'

'Is there anything in your rules that says I can't be drunk to do the deed? If I had a bottle of brandy—'

Impatiently, Carnivean snapped at one of his acolytes. 'Fetch a chalice and a bottle of brandy. And be quick about it.'

A black-hooded man hurried off towards a narrow passageway, returning moments later with brandy and a large chalice which he handed to Brakway, who put down the knife, unscrewed the top of the brandy and poured half the bottle into the chalice.

Pelhambury sniggered. 'First the unholy grail,' he said. 'And then the sacrifice.'

Brakway raised the chalice as if he might drink from it, but in one fluid movement he grabbed a candle from the nearest acolyte, threw the brandy at Ursula Pelhambury, and set light to her robe. She screamed as the flames bit into her body through the flimsy, flaming robe. As his wife screamed in agony, Pelhambury tried to smother her with his own body.

Holding the brandy bottle by the neck, Brakway sprayed an arc of the spirit across a wide circle of the evil Satanists, tilting the candlestick so that the robes of many of them went up in flames. In the ensuing chaos, Brakway used the knife to sever the young girl's ropes, grabbed her by the wrist, and dragged her towards the passageway, as the cries of burning pain echoed after them.

When he reached some double doors, he hurriedly flung them open and pushed the girl through. Behind the doors were two metal slots and he saw there was a long metal bar leaning against the wall. He slammed the doors shut and slotted the bar into the slots. There was now no way anyone could get out of the cave and follow them.

He entered the bar through the sliding door, holding tight to the girl's wrist, dragging her along. She seemed reluctant to go with him. He realised she was naked and quickly scanned the bar for anything to cover her nakedness. Where Pelhambury's wife had sat there was a red cashmere coat.

'Put this on,' he told the girl.

'Yes, but—' she began.

'Do it!' he yelled. 'And let's get out of here.'

He realised she was probably shocked and confused, so he threw the coat over her shoulders, and dragged her towards the main door. Luckily, his car keys were in his trouser pocket. He aimed the remote towards the Renault, heard the click and saw the lights flicker as the door locks were released. He opened the passenger door and shoved the girl inside. There was no time to put her seat belt on, so he dashed around to the driver's side and got in.

He switched the ignition on. 'Put your seat belt on,' he instructed her as he clipped his own into the buckle.

She obeyed his instruction, and he was relieved when he heard the click of her belt in its buckle. Now all he needed to do was get down the mountain as quickly as possible and call the police. An image of helpless people, burning in the cave as they tried to put out the fires, gave him mixed feelings of guilt and satisfaction.

To hell with them, he thought, and was almost amused by the irony of his thinking.

He was about to throw the car into gear when he saw a face at the pub window. He recognised the goatee beard and the sallow face. It was Carnivean. But how had he escaped from the cave?

'How the hell did Carnivean get out of there?' he said.

The girl next to him smiled and said, 'He's not like other people.'

And then Brakway watched as the face disappeared from the window. But what he didn't see was the landlord taking burning logs from the fireplace and setting the furniture alight.

Soon the pub was ablaze, but Brakway was already half a mile away by then, thinking about what he would tell the police, and the phone call to his old editor with the most sensational exclusive story of his career.

Another half mile down the mountain, Brakway remembered that soon there was the most treacherous hairpin bend coming up, and he gave the road his full attention. And then, only ten yards from the bend, the girl grabbed hold of the steering wheel and held it tight in one position. As they hurtled toward the hairpin bend, Brakway was unable to turn the wheel.

'What are you doing?' he screamed. It was then he realised the girl was possessed.

But the realisation came too late as the car hurtled over the edge of the road, and for a moment it sailed through space, before crashing into rocks, rolling and falling over a steep cliff, smashed into a jagged rock below, where the petrol tank was ruptured. It became a fireball as the fuel ignited and it fell another hundred feet into the valley below and exploded.

In the Eagle, regulars saw the explosion, and also noticed the distant flickering as the Lamb's fire raged high up in the mountain. Someone called the emergency services, but the fire engines had to come from the main county town, which would take at least half an hour. By then the pub would be razed to the ground.

In all the excitement, no one noticed the minibus, its headlights switched off, as it turned from the mountain road and headed away from the town, driven by its single occupant, a man with a goatee beard.

As for Brakway, ironically, he got his sensational story, though it was posthumous and far from exclusive.

4: Slugs

I was slightly hungover when I woke up that Sunday morning and saw my first slug. Disgusting it was. So slimy it made me feel nauseous, and that silver trail across the carpet was repulsive. I controlled the sickening lurch in my stomach by swallowing saliva.

I jumped out of bed, stepped over the revolting fat creature, careful to avoid its nauseating trail of silvery snot-like filth. I went into the kitchen and got a dustpan and brush, came back to the bedroom and swept it up. As I brushed it on to the dustpan, I saw it contract as my brush made contact, and then as it lay on the dustpan, it bloated itself again. Fat and obscene. I felt repulsed by it and placed the dustpan on the floor. As I wasn't dressed I had to quickly put my dressing gown and slippers on, all the while watching the slug from the corner of my eye in case it moved back onto the carpet from the dustpan. It had moved maybe an inch towards the carpet by the time I'd got my slippers on. I felt I was hyperventilating and could feel a headache coming on.

I lived in the ground floor flat, and that probably explained why the slug somehow got in from the communal garden. I took the dustpan with the revolting slug outside and jerked it forcefully towards the large hedge outside the front door, I saw the slimy creature hit the leaves and drop onto the concrete path. I shivered and prayed the awful creature couldn't crawl its way across the path and find some vent in the building giving it access to my flat again.

***

When I woke up the next day, the first thing I saw as I blinked my eyes into focus, was a silver trail across the carpet, running from the skirting board near the door and disappearing under my bed. I shuddered at the thought of this repulsive thing pulsing beneath me like a lump of solid mucus. Was this the same slug I wondered, and had it slithered back into my bedroom to torment me.

I stepped cautiously out of bed, in case it might be lurking just inches away, although I was level-headed enough to understand that slugs do not move rapidly. So, first I dropped onto my knees and peered under the bed, expecting to see the revolting slimy creature secreted in the dark, perhaps peering at me through its antennae and making me feel nauseous. But I couldn't see anything that looked like that revolting lump of shit. The slimy trail disappeared under the bed, and I could see nothing other than strands of dusty debris. What had happened to the slug? And then I felt a shard of icy fear stabbing me in the back. Supposing the slug had somehow managed to climb up and into the mattress? It was such a sickening thought my entire body shook.

I grabbed my dressing gown from the hook behind the door and got my slippers from under the chair. At least I felt less vulnerable as I was no longer naked. I knew little about slugs, other than keen gardeners hate them and put down slug pellets to keep them off their prize flowers, so I wasn't certain if they could climb or not. I didn't think so, but I was just guessing.

I pushed the bed over to one side, and looked down at the silver trail, which stopped just where the middle of the bed would have been. There was no slug. And it was at least two inches from the floor to the bottom of the bed. Surely it was not possible for a slug to leap up into the bed, and then – even supposing it could – it would have to crawl its way through the mattress. No. The slug trail stopped and there was no sign of the creature.

It was mysterious. I didn't know whether slugs could stop secreting their oily mucus membrane? If that was the case, this was even worse than finding the slimy trail, because if a slug could creep up on me like that...

Just to make certain the slug hadn't somehow got into the bed, I removed the bedclothes and checked the mattress. Nothing. The slug had disappeared where the trail ended. I remade the bed, then got a dishcloth and wiped away the trail before I slid the bed back into place.

I tried to forget the slug, but it lurked in my brain like a malignant being, and I could imagine large tentacles protruding from its slimy mass.

***

As a freelance management consultant, I had a month free of work, and felt I had to get out of the flat. I went for a long walk, killing time before going to the pub for the lunchtime session. When I got back to the flat later that afternoon, I checked the bedroom. No slug and no trail. I was so relieved I felt tears of relief clouding my eyes. Perhaps I had seen the last of the slug. Maybe it was just a freak incident. Just to make sure, I went around the room, checking the skirting board, but there seemed to be no gaps anywhere, no small holes.

When I mentioned a slug appearing in my bedroom to someone in the pub, I was told they can elongate themselves flat and can get through tiny gaps. Telling me this did not help.

Salt, I was told, does the trick. Slugs do not respond well to salt. I had one small salt cellar with possibly the equivalent of a tablespoon left in it, so I carefully shook a thin string of salt along the edge of the skirting board. I slept better that night, knowing any slugs were unlikely to cross the salt barrier.

***

When I woke the next day, imagine my horror when I saw there were now two slugs crossing the carpet, along the side of the bed – the side I usually get out of. I was so angry, I wanted to scream. I suppose it was because I felt so helpless. How could these hideous things ruin my day? The entire day, because I was aware that I would be thinking of them all the time and wouldn't be able to relax. The salt barrier hadn't worked, or maybe I needed more salt, masses of the stuff.

I didn't bother to shower and quickly got dressed in the previous day's clothes. Then I swept the slugs into the dustpan and disposed of them at the bottom of the garden.

I spotted the man in the first-floor flat staring out of his kitchen window, probably wondering what I was up to. I waved to him, but he didn't respond, probably embarrassed because I had caught him being nosy.

I drove to the supermarket that morning and bought three large canisters of salt. *That should do the trick, you little bastards,* I thought. When I got home, I poured mounds of salt all around the bedroom. I didn't care how unattractive it looked if it worked. The salt could stay where it was for months. I was quite willing to leave the salt there permanently. Anything was better than slugs and their ghastly mucus trails.

***

That same night, as I lay in bed, I became obsessed, and fearful of the slugs. I couldn't sleep. I imagined them somehow burrowing under the mounds of salt like prisoners of war escaping from camps. My imagination ran riot, and I kept telling myself that I was being stupid. Eventually, unable to get a wink of sleep, I switched on the bedside light.

There they were! Slugs! Six of them. Fat as pork sausages. But then I noticed a seventh slug by the skirting board, a yellowing mess like a pool of egg vomit, lying across a mound of salt, liquefied in its attempt to climb over or through it. I shuddered and gagged. And then I looked at the other six slugs, all healthy specimens, and wondered how they had survived the salt barricade.

I pulled back the duvet and stood up on the bed, putting as much distance as I could between me and the stomach-churning slugs, those lumps of excrement. I remained frozen, wondering how I was going to avoid them to get my dressing gown from behind the door. Avoiding them would be like weaving my way through a minefield, and the thoughts of the soles of my feet touching those foul freaks of nature filled me with such repugnance that I wanted smash my head against the wall.

And then I heard something. Coming from the slugs. I swear it was a noise like someone breathing. Very faint, but I was very still as I listened, straining to hear the slightest sigh. It was an indistinct sound I heard, like the exhalation of a breath, and I could have sworn the loathsome devils were communicating with each other. As I strained to hear the undefined breathing, I thought I saw the antennae of several of them waving. And I knew for certain that these disgusting lumps of useless matter were transmitting messages. I felt sick and scared and I knew I had to get out of there.

I balanced on the edge of the bed, saw there was a circle of slugs on the carpet between the bed and the door, with a small round area in the middle. If I manged to keep my balance, I thought, I could with one movement step into that area without touching any of the revolting things. I took a deep breath, stepped off the bed into the middle of the slug circle, and managed to grab my dressing gown. But as I swung open the living room door, I felt a ghastly, cold and jelly-like slug touching my right heel. Repelled and disgusted, I yelled with alarm as I darted into the lounge. And that was when I got the next nasty shock.

I could see mucus trails across the carpet, leading from beneath the front window to the bedroom door. So that was how the grotesque bastards had managed to avoid the salt, with one exception.

Hurriedly, I went into my small galley kitchen and removed the plastic bag containing rubbish from inside the small rubbish bin, grabbed a wire brush from under the sink, went back to the bedroom and swept all six slugs into the bin. Then I dashed barefoot into the garden and tipped the slugs into the compost heap.

I remembered the pub customer telling me that slugs like to eat rotting matter, and I hoped the compost heap would keep them happy for some time.

Still, I didn't want to take any chances, and so I bought more salt and distributed great piles of it under the window in the lounge and along the skirting board.

***

I still felt insecure. Vulnerable. So that night I slept in a pair of jeans and a shirt and kept a pair of slip-on shoes by my side on the bed. The trauma of the slugs on the previous day must have exhausted me because it took me ages to get to sleep, but when I did eventually drift off, I slept for at least seven hours. When I opened my eyes, I saw by the bedside alarm that it was gone nine-thirty. I must have been in a very deep sleep because I felt disorientated, the same feeling I got if I spent the night in a strange bed. And I had forgotten about the slugs. But as I began to adjust to my surroundings, I suddenly remembered the repulsive lumps of faecal matter polluting my bedroom last night. I raised my head to check the floor.

Jesus Christ! Palpitations of disgust shook me like a helpless ragdoll and cold terrors gripped me by the throat. I couldn't believe what I was seeing. I had put barricades of salt everywhere, but now the floor was covered in a carpet of slime. There must have been hundreds of the things. My bedroom was a blanket covering of slugs, and the sound of breathing from this pulsating mass was now a discharge of exhaled noise, a steady and deadly sighing.

I had to get out of there. But there was no way I could make the lounge and not tread on this slithering mass of vile contamination. I grabbed my shoes and slipped them on hurriedly, then stood up and perched on the end of the bed, facing the door. That was when I knew they were out to get me, those demons, sent by some evil entity. There was only one way I could think of to survive and triumph over this monstrous instrument of demonic forces.

I leapt off the bed, feeling the disgusting squelch of the slugs beneath the soles of my shoes. I threw open the door, grabbed my cigarette lighter and car keys from the kitchen hook and rushed out into the garden car park. I opened the boot and got out the spare can of petrol. I was panicking. As I dashed back indoors, unscrewing the petrol cap on the plastic container, I spilt a stream of it as I came back into the flat. I opened the bedroom door and doused the slugs with nearly five litres of petrol. I lit the cigarette lighter and chucked it on to the mass of flammable slugs. It was exhilarating. There was a great whoosh as the bedroom caught fire, and I thought I heard a banshee scream as the slugs went up in flames. It didn't matter that the flat was now a conflagration as the bed and all the clothing caught fire with another great crackling whoosh. The fire was wonderful. It cleansed and destroyed. All the filth and slime destroyed. Cleansed by that magnificent fire.

***

Another session with the doctor today. We talked about the fire. And why the man in the flat upstairs didn't get out in time. How was I to know he was unemployed and still in bed when the fire started? It was because I spilt petrol in the communal hallway that the fire spread beyond my flat. I had to get out through the front window. The fire was unfortunate, intended as a purifying measure. And it wasn't my fault the flat was contaminated with those demonic slugs. I had to disinfect the flat, didn't I? And the fire sanitized it. Otherwise the evil would have spread. But I don't think they understood my reason. The way they stared at me. I just couldn't make them understand. Which is why I was charged with manslaughter. And when I tried to explain about the evil slugs, I was put in this place.

How long am I here for? I asked the doctor. And he told me there was no date set for my release. And there might not be for some time, he said. Probably not for— He waved a hand carelessly and didn't finish what he was going to say.

I quite like the doctor. A very sympathetic person. He seems to understand about the slugs and the fire. When I told him about the sausages we had for lunch, which reminded me of slugs, and I threw a fit and had to be restrained, he was quite gentle and understanding later. And now he has promised me that in future none of my food will ever look like slugs.

Which doesn't solve the problem of that fat female nurse. She has bloated smooth skin, and her eyebrows remind me of antennae. And her body makes me shiver, as I imagine her slithering across the highly polished floor, leaving behind a slimy trail.

So now I am waiting.

Waiting to slit her throat.

With that razor blade I found in the waste-bin.

I'm sure when I get rid of her the doctor will understand.

The opportunity presented itself a day later as she came to give me my medication. As she leaned over me, I could smell her breath, rancid and disgusting, as if her body inside bubbled and oozed with an amoeba-like jelly. She turned my stomach. Then, in that briefest of moments, I grabbed her by the hair and slashed her throat with the razor, the other side of the blade cutting into my fingers, but I didn't care. Any pain was better than having this monstrous slug hanging over me. She made a slug gurgling noise as the ghastly liquid spurted from her neck.

Then I felt hands grabbing me, shoving me into that tight-fitting jacket.

Later, much later, still encumbered by the harsh jacket, I was interviewed by the doctor. I was silent. I didn't answer any of his questions.

I don't know how long it has been since I've spoken. Months? Years, even. But although I quite like the doctor, lately he seems to have put on weight. I stare at him sometimes and shiver. His jowls are too fleshy now, and his cheeks are loose and rubbery. I'm starting to find him repugnant.

He has become slug-like, and I know I must destroy him.

Now it has become a waiting game. I will bide my time. But I must kill all the slugs. It is my duty. I will be performing a service to mankind. Yes, the slug-doctor will have to be destroyed. It's just a matter of time.

5: Evil Answers Evil

The tribunal consisted of three judges, and the name of each man of this triumvirate was secret. They could only be known as Judges One, Two and Three for reasons of security. In any case, it would have been difficult to tell them apart. They wore identical robes, all the same off-white colour, and their beards and moustaches were neither too long and bushy nor too short and embellishing.

The court was packed and there were many cases to adjudicate. The judges were perceived to be objective and wise, otherwise how else would they have reached this important height of authority? The first case that morning was the trial of a young student, who had flouted the internal internet laws and used secret software to contact forbidden websites. The case was dispensed with speedily and the culprit was given a five-year jail sentence, which was considered lenient, as the offender might be paroled after three years if the prison authorities thought she was genuinely contrite and understood the gravity of contacting decadent countries. The second trial was of a woman who had been exposed by an anonymous informant and found to be secretly wearing black-market make-up and listening to smuggled pop records. This crime was considered so grave that the judges unanimously agreed to commit her to ten years' hard labour. The young woman left the court, numb and fighting back tears, because to openly cry and wail was considered a criticism of the judges' ruling and could incur years more added to the sentence. There were murmurs in the courtroom that the judges were justly benevolent and must have been in an unusually good mood for not imposing fifty lashes on the woman prior to the start of her sentence.

The third trial of the morning was of a middle-aged man, represented by an advocate, his spiritual leader. The defendant was scruffily dressed, with a sallow face and scrawny build, and shoulders burdened by foregone defeat. His spiritual leader was tall and imposing, with a beard that reached his breastbone. The defendant's crime was considered one of the worst, second only to murder. Theft. And this man had not just stolen food to feed his family, he had stolen gold and jewellery from a store near the marketplace. Even to steal food was bad enough, but to profit from stealing luxury items there would be a crime-fitting punishment, which the defendant feared with a terrifying numbness, his brain and body having given up the will to live.

Although the judges pointed out that had the accused stolen bread to feed his family – which of course they could not condone – it might not be considered as morally wrong as the theft of the jewellery, which was a reprehensible crime, one for which the severest sentence would be imposed. The defendant's advocate argued that it was his client's intention to sell the gold and jewellery to raise money to feed his family, and there was little difference between stealing these items and the theft of food, because clearly his motive was the need to fend off starvation for both himself and family. This simple argument had never been put before the court before, and the judges decided on a ten-minute recess to consider the argument. During the break in the proceedings, the argument was discussed hurriedly, because there were many cases to get through that morning. Judges One and Two were in favour of a harsh punishment, which would act as a deterrent to any other citizens who might be tempted to steal luxury items. The motive for the theft was irrelevant, they argued. But Judge Three was more compassionate than his colleagues and appealed for leniency. He asked that the accused be sentenced to nothing more than one-hundred lashes and a prison sentence. But the other two judges were adamant that the punishment should fit the crime, as the law stated. It was also the law that a tribunal had to reach a decision on a two against one basis, unless the one in disagreement could persuade one of the other two judges to convert. This Judge Three failed to do.

When, after the brief recess, they returned to the court, the accused stared at them fearfully, and his legs turned to jelly. Although the judges' expressions were inscrutable, he thought he detected a mixture of sorrow and remorse in Judge Three's eyes, and he knew from this small sign that his fate was decided.

Judge One glanced at his watch before proceeding with the sentence, knowing they still had many cases to resolve before midday and he was due to play golf with an influential oilman later that afternoon. He, therefore, resolved not to make a speech and pronounced the sentence dismissively.

The accused was sentenced to a right-hand amputation, the ultimate punishment for theft.

Although other meddling countries considered sentences such as these to be barbaric, it was asserted in defence of this law that these sentences were administered humanely, and the accused was taken to a hospital where the operation was carried out by a surgeon.

As an unskilled worker with both his hands, the man barely earned a living for himself and his family with badly-paid labouring jobs. Now, after the amputation, he found it impossible to work. Nobody wanted to employ a one-handed labourer, even in the most menial of tasks. He was reduced to begging, but the pathetic alms dropped into his begging bowl amounted to less than enough to keep his family alive. Despairing, and having reached the end of expectation and faith, he resolved to end the pain of living. Towards the end of one blisteringly hot day spent begging in the market-place, he stared at the few coins in his begging bowl and knew what he must do. He found an empty plastic bottle and spent the money begged on half a litre of petrol at a garage. That same night, having made certain his wife and three young children were fast asleep, he emptied the bottle of petrol around their one room, careful not to wake his family. In the past, optimistically believing in a just and benevolent God, who might one day alter his destiny and sustain him, he now rejected the supreme being, changing his allegiance. He prayed to the devil for revenge, cursing the judges and the regime of his country; and, minutes before lighting the fire, his brain spewed devil's curses on them. Evil answers evil, a devil voice screamed in his head. As he committed his soul to the devil in exchange for revenge, he lit the fire.

Their small abode was razed to the ground within minutes, and the one-handed labourer, his wife and family perished in the fire. It was said by neighbours that he couldn't live with the humiliation of the theft, and the amputated hand was a stigma and constant reminder of his crime. Although some neighbours were sympathetic towards his suicide, others condemned him for killing his innocent children.

At the hospital, his right hand lay in a pile of body parts in a metal container waiting to be incinerated. As the furnace blazed, the hand squeezed through severed arms, kidneys, feet, legs, livers, entrails, and wriggled through the body parts until it reached the top of the container. It pulled itself over the rim and dropped to the floor with a soft squelching sound, then scurried, spider-like to a dark corner just as a hospital porter entered the furnace room. Thinking he had seen something from the corner of his eye, the porter walked towards an air vent in the floor. He couldn't see anything. Either he was mistaken, or it was an insect of some sort.

***

Judge One lived in a luxurious ten-bedroom house which he shared with two wives and seven children. Two nights after the amputee's suicide, and sleeping soundly in his own master bedroom, Judge One woke suddenly and heard a scuffling sound outside his door. He thought it might be his youngest child wanting a story and a cuddle from his father, which he occasionally did, and being the youngest and the only boy, he was invariably indulged by his father.

Judge One got out of bed and tiptoed to the door. He was surprised to find there was no one there. Thinking he must have dreamt it, he closed the door and returned to his bed. But now the scuffling sound seemed to be coming from somewhere inside the bedroom. The window, with a view of the resplendent garden, was wide open, and a breeze blew the diaphanous curtains high in the room. Thinking the scuffling he heard was nothing more than the curtain material brushing against the window frame, he turned over and closed his eyes.

That was when he was disturbed by a crawling noise, the sound of a giant insect creeping across the rug near the window. He sat bolt upright and looked down at the floor, thinking he could see the silhouette of a rat scuttling across the floor. It disappeared under the bed.

His breath froze in his chest. He wasn't a man who was easily frightened, but there was something deeply sinister about the shadow of the thing he had glimpsed briefly. He sat listening for any sound from under the bed, feeling vulnerable as the creature was now beneath him. He hated rats, they sickened him, and he shuddered with repulsion.

Of course, he could call out for one of the servants to deal with it. But that would involve disturbing the household, and if it turned out to be a false alarm, he would appear foolish. He waited. Listening. His ears straining for the slightest sound in the dark. But there was nothing.

Because it was dark, he thought perhaps he was mistaken, and whatever he had seen had probably been magnified by his imagination and was nothing more than a large cockroach.

He knew he couldn't ignore whatever was under the bed and go back to sleep. He would have to deal with it. He was about to reach for the bedside light when there was a slight scraping noise, a scratching sound, like a fingernail on material. He froze, and a helpless fear poisoned his brain. Unable to move, he dreaded what lay beneath him? He tried to swallow, but his mouth was too dry. There was definitely something there. Right under him.

Another voice in his head told him he was being ridiculous. A grown man, scared of an insect or a rodent, however large, was shameful. He heard an echoing laugh in his mind, an accusing jeer, charging him with cowardice.

Determined to deal with it, he switched on the bedside light. The heavily-shaded bulb threw out a soft light, more of a glow than a brightness. He stared at the rug for a moment, as if he expected to see evidence of an insect or rodent, a trail of some sort, but there was nothing. He turned and eased his feet out of bed, stepping as far away from the bed as he could reach, then padded across the room, slid open one of his wardrobe doors and picked up a shoe with which to swat the rodent, or whatever it was that lurked beneath his bed.

Shivering with fearful anticipation, he knelt at the end of the bed, took a deep breath to prepare himself for what he might find, and gripped the shoe tightly in his right hand as he carefully raised the valence, turning his head side-on to see what was under the bed.

The scream stuck in his throat as the severed hand scurried towards him and grabbed him by the throat. He fell backwards and let go of the shoe as he tried to pull the choking hand away from his neck. But the grip was too powerful. The fingers were like leather straps tightening around his throat, cutting the skin. He couldn't breathe. The fingers closed around his neck like a vice. He wanted to cry for help, but his scream was no more than a hoarse gasp. He tried to breathe but the hand was too tough, cutting off the air, and closing tighter and tighter around his neck. As he started to black out the hand released its grip on his throat, and the fingers crawled quickly across his face, sunk thumb and index finger into his right eye, took hold of the eyeball and yanked it away from its socket. The judge, who was semi-conscious, cried out as the hand let go of the eyeball, dropped it on to the rug, then gripped his neck even tighter than before. From the judge's throat came a loud and choking rattle. His head went limp and he was dead in less than a minute. The hand released its grip, then scurried towards the window.

That same night Judge Two was working late while his family slept. Feeling tired from staring at the computer screen, he thought of reviving himself with a swim. His study opened out on to a large patio, garden and swimming pool. He removed his bathrobe and stepped out, took hold of the pool ladder, and was about to turn and lower himself into the water when he heard a scuffling noise from behind. He turned sharply, wondering if it was an animal of some sort that had crept into his study. And then he heard a faint clicking sound, a tap-tap on his computer keyboard. Thinking it might be one of his children having disobeyed his ruling about his study being out of bounds, he strode angrily into the study, brushing aside the curtains. The tapping stopped, and there was nothing to be seen.

Judge Two wiped his brow. Perhaps he was overworked. He sighed, shook his head and returned to the edge of the pool. But there it was again! There was no mistaking that sound of tapping on the keyboard.

He froze, listening to the confident sound of someone typing on his computer. Yet all he saw as he peered into his study was the back of the computer monitor. Had someone been sitting behind his desk, typing on the computer, he would see them. For a moment he was unable to move, as he listened to the clacking of the keyboard. Perhaps he imagined it. Cautiously, he walked slowly back into his study. The keyboard tapping stopped as soon as he entered. He circled his desk warily, then stopped to stare at the computer monitor. There was no one in the room, and yet someone had written a message three times. The messages read:

EVIL ANSWERS EVIL. EVIL ANSWERS EVIL. EVIL ANSWERS EVIL.

What could it mean? And how did the message get there? Perhaps, thought the judge, tugging his beard thoughtfully, it came via the internet, sent by a hacker. A radical. One of those fanatical left-wing extremists.

Then, out of the corner of his eye, he saw something slithering towards the window. It looked like a small rodent. Grabbing a club from his golf bag in a corner of the room, he hurried out on to the patio, determined to bludgeon the creature, smash it to a pulp. Breathing heavily, he surveyed the patio and garden. But, apart from the gentle rippling of the water in the pool, nothing moved. He stood still, listening. All was quiet. Had he imagined the rodent? Perhaps it was his mind playing tricks because of his exhaustion. Clearly, he had overdone the work and was now too fatigued to think straight. A swim would wake him up and clear his mind.

He lay the golf club on a sun lounger, and stepped onto the pool ladder, easing himself into the cool, refreshing water. He was up to his neck in water when he heard a scuffling sound from the top of the ladder. Looking up, he saw the shape of a hand, which suddenly dropped onto his head, the fingers scratching and clawing at his face. As the hideous creature dug nails like talons into his eyes, he thrashed about, choking and fighting for his life. And then the fingers buried deep into his right eye, tugging at his eyeball. He tried to scream, but his mouth was under the surface. He tried to breathe, but his mouth filled with water. Choking and spluttering, he felt his eyeball being wrenched from its socket. And then, as he tried to raise his head above the surface, the hand pushed his head back under, and water filled his lungs.

It was almost dawn and the sky was brightening rapidly. From Judge Two's garden came a light scampering sound and a shadow flitted across the ground and disappeared beneath a small gap in the garden wall. The judge floated face down in the pool, while his right eye gazed lifelessly at the fading stars above.

***

When the judges' corpses were discovered, and police were called to investigate the atrocity, it was decided by the upper echelons of the elite forces of law and order that the mysterious killings should not be made public, as they were wary of humiliating the ruling classes in any way, exposing them to a vulnerability shared by the masses. The investigating officers tasked with solving the crimes were hand-picked detectives who worked exclusively for the monarchy, and these highly-trained praetorian guards were fanatically loyal to their rulers. However, it was decided that Judge Three should be informed of the tragic circumstances of his colleagues' bizarre killings, so that he could take necessary steps to protect himself. But when he demanded police protection, this was refused, and no reason was given. Instead, they issued him with a pistol, and he was also given intensive target practice at a shooting gallery. Now he was trained and armed, he felt indestructible. After all, the murders of his colleagues looked like nothing more than the work of a lunatic with a grudge. Which was why, he reasoned, the authorities denied him police protection, knowing he could deal with it himself.

The night after the death of his colleagues, Judge Three chose to sleep alone in the master bedroom, the pistol beside him on the bedside table. Upon retiring at midnight, he made certain the door and windows were shut tight and locked, so that there was no way any intruder could secure entry into his space. What he failed to see as he bolted the door and windows, was that his bedroom was already occupied by an intruder, and the infiltrator was hidden behind an armchair, waiting for its victim to settle down for the night. As soon as the judge climbed into bed and switched off the light, confident his territory was secure from invasion, he nevertheless felt a slight tremor of nervousness. Reaching out in the dark, he felt for the gun on his bedside table, and released the safety catch. He tapped the weapon almost affectionately, and permitted himself a smile, feeling immune from danger now.

He lay back, pulling the bedsheet around himself and closed his eyes. But now he felt wide awake. Unable to settle down. He shifted and turned, and the arms of his pyjama top felt irritatingly tight under his arms every time he moved. Exasperated by his inability to get comfortable, he tried to relax, but still he felt distraught. He thought about the other two judges, colleagues and friends of his, who had somehow become the victims of a murdering lunatic.

And then, unable to sleep, his mind explored and wandered dark avenues, making connections to recent events. He thought about the poor labourer, and how he had been unable to change one of his colleagues' opinions to give the man a custodial sentence instead of an amputation. Perhaps he should have argued more convincingly, but he had a function to attend that same afternoon and wanted to get the sentence over and done with quickly. And, in any case, the way the sentence had been decided was the law. And the law had to be obeyed. In any case, Judge Three concluded in his drowsy state, the man was a thief, and the sentence was justified by the crime.

He yawned loudly, feeling sleepy now, and began to breathe evenly, his head pressed deep into the pillow.

And then he heard a scampering sound, softly at first, then getting louder as something shuffled across the floor. Or was it his imagination? The door was securely bolted from the inside, and the windows were locked. Nobody could get inside his bedroom. He must have imagined it. He felt a rustling noise, a swishing sound from the sheet that hung over the side of the bed. Something was climbing up onto the bed. He reached for the gun, and as his fingers slid over the metal, claw-like fingers grabbed the back of his neck. Yelling in fear, he leapt out of bed, and turned, trying to aim the gun towards the bed. But it was dark, and he couldn't see anything, not the shadow of an intruder. Nothing.

He felt ghastly fingers grabbing his pyjama trousers as the creature climbed up his leg, and then a hand clutched his genitals. The pain was unbelievably intense as his testicles were squeezed so tight he thought they would burst, and he might pass out with the pain. He had the gun aimed at the thing that clutched him, but he couldn't risk shooting himself. He cried out and begged for mercy, crying for the acute pain to cease. And then the hand released its grip and he fell in a heap on the floor, his hands holding his genitals, trying to ease the throbbing, shooting pain, his body a dreadful spasm of suffering. The pain was so intense in his testicles he barely noticed the hand sliding over his face. He screamed in fear and agony as he felt in his right eye the fingers grabbing and pulling at his eyeball.

His agonized scream woke the household. And then it was silenced by a single shot.

***

The family, when they managed to force open the door, found him lying on the floor next to the bed, the gun close to his hand, having died from a single shot to the head. It looked like suicide, but for the blinding of his right eye.

After the police were called, the case was soon handed over to the elite forces of the monarchy. At first they admitted it looked like a suicide, but there was still the suspicion that it might be murder, mainly because of the copy-cat mutilation of the right eye like that of the other two judges.

The question remained though, the officer in charge pondered, of how the perpetrator – if it was a murder – got inside the room when the windows were locked, and the door was bolted from the inside. When he questioned the family, they admitted no one could bear to be in the same room as the corpse with its hideous empty eye socket, the grotesque eyeball, and the blood spatters on the wall and rug from the gunshot, and so they had left the room empty while they called the police. The officer surmised, once he learned that the judge hadn't gone into his room until midnight, that a perpetrator could have entered at any time before midnight, concealed himself in the room, committed the crime, hid in the built-in wardrobe, and after the body was discovered and the relatives left the room, made his escape. But when the officer's forensic expert checked the gun for fingerprints, prints on the gun were found not to match those of the judge. And when they checked their criminal fingerprint data base, there was no match.

But it still looked as if a mysterious perpetrator was involved in all three deaths, because prints taken from Judge Two's computer keyboard matched the fingerprints on Judge Three's gun.

Once the evidence had been hastily scrutinized, a decision was reached by the ruling elite in less than six hours. The case was recorded as a bizarre suicide pact where all three judges plucked out their own eyes. It was officially stated that Judge One intended committing suicide and plucking out his own eye brought on a heart attack which proved fatal. Judge Two plucked out his eye in the swimming pool and deliberately drowned himself. And Judge Three plucked out his eye and then shot himself.

Details of the fingerprints were expunged from the records, as was the message on Judge Two's computer. Given that such a mystery could never be satisfactorily resolved, it was decided by the powers-that-be that it was safer to bury the case. It was now considered highly confidential and was airbrushed from the records.

The judges' families were given the verdicts of the bizarre deaths and ordered never to speak to anyone about the case for fear losing certain privileges – or worse.

***

The porter wheeled more body parts into the incineration unit. He pushed the trolley through the swing doors and wheeled it towards the large container which was now almost overflowing with human flesh and bones. He lifted the small container on his trolley, which contained the remains of recent operations, and tipped it into the large container.

He checked the temperature on the thermostat and decided it was now high enough to turn everything quickly into ash. He wheeled the container towards the door of the incinerator, made certain his protective gloves were comfortably tight on his hands, then turned his back on the container. He was about to turn the lever to open the door of the incinerator when his foot caught something on the concrete floor. Frowning, he looked down at the hand, wondering how it got there. He didn't remember it falling out of the container or off the trolley. It must have happened while he was about to open the incinerator door, he decided. He bent over and picked it up. He was about to throw it on to the container when he noticed a small scar on the back of the hand. His frown deepened. It looked like the hand of that thief, the thief whose punishment was amputation. But that sentence was carried out almost two weeks ago. He was sure of it. There had been a small scar which ran from the wrist diagonally across the back of the hand from the left towards the little finger. It looked as if a tool like a chisel had been used, slipped, and caused the wound. But how had this body part become overlooked? Perhaps, thought the porter, the hand had fallen off the overfull container and somehow become concealed beneath one of the other trolleys. It was strange, he thought, how he had supervised many incinerations since then, and if the hand had somehow fallen out of the container, how was it he had never noticed it until now? He was usually so careful, dedicated in his job. How had he managed to drop this body part from the container? He shrugged, dismissing it as one of life's unsolvable mysteries, like forgetting where one has left one's keys or reading glasses. Thinking no more about the hand, and the thief's cruel sentence, he threw it into the container, then turned away and opened the incinerator door. He felt the blast of heat, and immediately sweat broke out on his forehead and under his arms.

When he turned back and was about to tip the container into the furnace, he could have sworn the hand was on top of the pile. But the heat now was unbearable, so he dismissed further thoughts of the hand and tipped the body parts into the furnace. A loud crackle and sizzling sound as they burned, and as he inhaled the familiar smell of roasting flesh, he thought he saw out of the corner of his eye a rat scampering across the floor towards the swing doors.

Quickly he slammed the incinerator door shut, picked up a heavy metal rod and went after the rat. He pushed through the swing doors, and at the end of the corridor, where the stairs leading to some of the wards were, he thought he saw the rat rounding the corner and heard the scampering of feet on concrete. Panicking, he knew he had to destroy the rat, but how would it look if he appeared in one of the hospital wards brandishing a lethal weapon? He dropped the metal rod and hurried after the rat, thinking he might catch it with his gloved hands and break its neck.

But having searched the wards thoroughly he saw nothing of the rat, which somehow must have escaped outside the hospital. After his shift ended that evening and he went home, he was sullen, and when his wife asked him what was wrong, he couldn't give any explanation for his mood, and she ignored it, thinking it might be a symptom of overwork.

That night, as he lay in bed next to his wife, he thought he heard a scurrying noise. His eyes flew open in alarm, and he saw poised above him, like an evil angel of death, a hand hovering close to his face. Suddenly the hand dropped, covering his hand and nose, smothering him. He couldn't breathe, and he struggled to prise off the hand, the fingernails digging into his cheeks like sharp talons.

He screamed, a blood-curdling cry of pain, which woke his wife and children. He shook and sweated, until his wife calmed him, dabbing his forehead with a corner of her nightdress, and reassured the children that their father had merely suffered a terrible nightmare.

When he got to work the next day, he discovered cordons of police everywhere. Apparently the Justice Secretary of the State, reclining in one of the private rooms for a minor operation had been strangled, first having had both eyes pulled out and forcibly squeezed dry until they were almost unrecognisable as eyes.

The police interviewed the porter, who told them about the mysterious hand, and the rat incident, and even included his nightmare as evidence. He was rudely dismissed, but first warned that it would be dangerous for him to spread any ridiculous theories like that publicly, or the consequences would be severe.

The porter kept his word and told no one. But he was a superstitious man, and deep down he was convinced now that the hand was the devil's revenge and would continue to wreak havoc in their society. And he was glad that the hellish hand would kill and go on killing.

Perhaps it was only the beginning, and there was worse, much worse, to come.

Every time he thought about it, the porter laughed loudly. And his laughter became demonic, almost as if he had joined forces with the instrument of revenge. The fiendish hand.

6: Self-Portrait

Starts to rain as I walk along The Strand. Turn my collar up. Can't face the crowded train tonight, crammed in tight and smelling of damp clothes, faces with obscene mouths and sniffing noses. Last night's journey another nightmare. The man opposite asleep, mouth wide open like a scream, reminding me of that horrendous painting. Can't face another journey like that.

Rain heavier now as I walk through the arches of Somerset House, heading for the Courtauld Gallery before it closes. Hand over my money just before 5.30 and head straight for Vincent. And there he is, in his green jacket, cap and bandaged ear. The gallery will close in half an hour, so I stand and stare at poor van Gogh, seeing despair in his eyes, wondering yet again how he painted his portrait, confronting the mirror-image torment of his soul, sucking it out then smoothing it out with bright brushstrokes. And was there anger in the paint? Or did the colour soothe his savage disposition?

A tourist passes in front of me and I struggle to suppress an irrational rage. Get out of my way. Don't come between me and the man I'm trying to understand. And although the gallery is busy, and there is a smell of dripping raincoats mingled with sweat, the power of van Gogh's brushstrokes and bright colours means I can smell the paint. But I know it's an illusion, like the portrait. And then the announcement comes, and I know I must leave and head for the station. Slowly. To miss the overcrowded cattle-truck I caught last night and avoid those menacing cadaverous faces.

I walk along the Embankment. Rivulets of rain running down my neck beneath my collar, but I don't mind. This is physical and real, and nature can do its worst as far as I'm concerned. Cross the road to stare at the murky Thames, current swirling like a whirlpool, and again there are echoes of The Scream. Catch myself out in a shiver that has nothing to do with the reality of the cleansing rain but the thoughts of commuting. All that hostility in the stares of the commuters.

Missed three trains so far. Wander slowly up the hill to Charing Cross to catch the next. Should be fewer passengers by now.

Tomorrow is Friday. Soon have two whole days free before I do this stone-rolling penance again. But first the early morning commute to London with those vacant screaming faces, thoughts of the return journey tunnelling in my brain like a diseased worm.

Friday travel much worse, the morning train delayed by twenty minutes. More time spent shifting uncomfortably in my seat. Sitting next to overweight, broad-shouldered man who encroaches on my space. Can feel his elbows digging in my side. I want to scream, like the painting. I know how that fear paralyses you, just as I know what Vincent went through.

Glad to get to work. Left alone in the bowels of the institute, logging and collating. Alone, thank God. They leave me alone to get on with my work. Occasionally they try to engage me in conversation. I'm never rude but I make it clear that I'm not the sociable type. For lunch I don't move from my work-station, eat my sandwich, then get on with my collating. Finish work at five, and then comes the Friday rush to get home. Would like to visit the gallery again and see Vincent but I can't afford it. Been twice already this week. Will treat myself on Monday. But now I need to kill time to avoid the rush hour. No use trying to find an uncrowded pub. A pub in central London on a Friday evening is just as bad as the packed trains. Perhaps worse. So now I visit second-hand bookshops in Charing Cross Road and Cecil Court, browsing until they shut at six. Need to kill time until seven at least, when the trains not quite as bad. After the bookshops, wander through Leicester Square and watch the buskers from a distance. Starts to drizzle, and I shuffle back past Leicester Square Tube station and see the Salisbury pub in St Martin's Lane is not overcrowded. Find some space at the bar and order a large Pernod with ice, then realise that for just a few pounds more I could have done the Courtauld again. But the gallery shuts at six, so there would still be the problem of what to do until seven. Think I made the right decision. Although I would have liked to see Vincent again.

Later train tonight just as bad. Crammed in next to woman who keeps coughing. Staccato coughs just seconds apart. Feel my nails digging into my palms. Try to control myself, stop myself from screaming. All the way to Northfleet would drive me mad. But she gets off at Crayford. Northfleet only another five stops, and although the coughing woman has gone, I still can't relax.

Deep depression strikes me when I get home. I hate my stodgy flat. Immediately confront my easel. Glare at my latest painting. An amateur effort. I tell myself for the umpteenth time that serious artists do not live in Northfleet. Making excuses. And that excuse is confirmed when Jeremy visits. We met at art school. He stares at my painting. Expecting bad criticism, he confounds me. Tells me how good it is. We quarrel. I tell him what I think of his own efforts and he departs, slamming the door. Says we are finished as friends.

I know what I must do.

I go into the bathroom and stare at the mirror for a long time. Just like Vincent and Gauguin, we are no longer friends but enemies. And just like Vincent I pick up the cutthroat razor. I'm right-handed like him. What was he thinking, I wonder, as he stared at his mirror image, his left ear bandaged? I open the razor, slide the blade out of its sheath. I do it angrily, like he did. Hack suddenly, blade slicing into flesh. Blood spurting across the mirror and dripping into the basin. The only pain I feel is his despair.

In my left hand a large chunk of my ear. Blood keeps pouring, running down my face and neck. Start to regret my volatile action. Blood won't stop. The chunk of my ear feels unreal, like someone else's ear. Catholics believe in transubstantiation, the very real flesh and blood of Christ. Not a symbol. Reality. Believe hard enough and it becomes a reality. Perhaps this really is van Gogh's ear in my hand. But the blood won't stop, so I wrap a towel round my head and call for a taxi.

It being Friday night, A & E is crowded. A policeman wants to know how I lost my ear. I lie. I tell him I was attacked in the street by a knife-wielding gang. He asks for a description, and I say they wore hoods.

Five hours later, my head bandaged just like Vincent, I go home. Stare into the mirror for a long time, wondering if I will ever see my friend again. And if he sees me like this, will he understand?

But I know who helps me to understand, and I will return on Monday evening to admire his portrait. Poor Vincent van Gogh. Just like me in so many ways. Did you ever smile? Did you ever laugh at a joke?

Or was life too harsh?

7: The Car from Hell

The incident happened at 10.00 a.m. one Saturday morning in early July, not long after PC Maggie Saunders's patrol shift began. She was partnered by PC Kevin Hughes, who was inexperienced and had not long graduated from police training academy. Maggie, being more experienced and four years older than the rookie policeman, tended to take charge, even though they were of equal rank.

That morning there had been a spate of burglaries, most of them reported by early-risers, who had discovered their garden sheds had been broken into, and all kinds of tools were reported stolen, although nothing electrical had been taken. By 9:30 there were reports of twelve shed burglaries, and there could well be many more, yet to be discovered by those who hadn't gone out to their back gardens.

Patrol car officers were told to keep a look out for any suspicious-looking vehicles, especially vans capable of carrying and concealing a substantial load of stolen goods. Alerted to the shed crimes, Maggie and Kevin, the latter driving, toured the area. but without much hope of arresting the culprit, suspecting that the thief – if it was a perpetrator working solo – would be long gone from the area by now.

Although they operated mainly in and on the outskirts of the town, and rarely cruised this far into the countryside, their rural excursion on this particular morning was in case they might light on any suspicious vehicles heading for the next county, the border of which was less than ten miles away and beyond their jurisdiction.

Maggie sighed deeply. 'I think this shed burglar will be long gone by now.'

'You think so?' Kevin questioned.

'Don't you?'

Kevin shrugged. Being new to the job, he was reluctant to offer opinions which could turn out to be wrong. He was cautious, wanting to prove himself, which Maggie found frustrating. She needed to talk, theorise, and conjecture. She felt brainstorming was one of the most effective ways of dealing with the day-to-day practice of policing. Most of their incidents were routine, dealing with domestic arguments and small-town drunken assaults. But Maggie was ambitious and motivated, and she could see her career blossoming in the future, rising from uniform to plain clothes. She longed for the challenge of detection and the solving of an occasional rape or murder.

She heard Kevin clearing his throat and wondered if he was about to offer an opinion about the burglaries. Instead, he said, rather incongruously, 'I've heard the Chateau Lyon is almost the same as one in France. Almost identical I've heard.'

'What are you on about, Kevin?'

'The hotel – half a mile up the road. Expensive it is. Over a fiver for a pint of ordinary. I wouldn't see the point of driving out here for a pint at that price.'

'The *point*,' Maggie emphasised, 'is that the Chateau Lyon is not like a pub, Kevin. It's for weddings and conferences. And you always pay over the odds in those places.'

Not far from the entrance to Chateau Lyon, a car pulled out in front of them, causing Kevin to slam his foot on the brakes. He cursed the driver, who must have noticed the police car following him, and put his foot down. Most drivers followed by a patrol car tend to do the opposite and slow to a crawl. Not this one, who suddenly accelerated from thirty to sixty in a matter of seconds.

'I think we ought to pull him over,' Maggie said.

And when they saw the car swerve erratically, Kevin agreed. 'I think you're right, Maggie. Looks like he was on a bender last night. We'll have him.'

Maggie switched on the siren and flashing lights while Kevin slammed his foot to the floor. There was a bend up ahead and they saw the car's brake lights come on. Kevin followed, taking the corner at speed, and they lessened the gap between their vehicle and the saloon car. And then the driver must have decided he would make things worse for himself if he ignored the police warning, and they saw the glare of his brake lights again as he slowed to a reasonable speed and allowed them to overtake him.

'There's a lay-by up ahead, indicate and we'll pull in there,' Maggie said breathlessly, roused by the thrill of the chase.

Kevin, also exhilarated by the sudden action, chuckled loudly. 'That was bloody convenient. Jesus Christ! Did you see the car number plate? K1LL6.'

'I think,' Maggie said, 'the second letter was a number one.'

'Even so. I hope it's not a personalised number plate.'

Maggie chuckled. 'Or it could be Satan who's at the wheel.'

'Yeah. I guess Satan would drive a luxury vehicle like this one. Looks like top of its range to me.'

A hundred yards further on, a large, dirty white van was parked in the lay-by and they pulled in behind it. The luxury car followed dutifully and glided to a stop behind them. As they got out of the patrol car, they could see the strained expression on the driver's face, bloated and red after a night of excess alcohol, and still well over the limit, probably.

Kevin reached the driver's side and gestured for the window to be lowered. The man, middle-aged and portly with grey, steel-wool hair, his forehead wet with perspiration, looked up at Kevin as the window slid down, and his expression said it all. He knew for certain this was going to be a driving ban. There was no emotion in his voice when he offered Kevin a lame excuse, as if he knew it was pointless but felt he had to say something.

'S-sorry. I didn't mean to pull out in front of you. I wasn't concentrating. It's been one of those mornings.'

Kevin looked down at him severely as he waited for Maggie to arrive at his side with the breathalyser, to take charge of the situation.

'You were also driving rather erratically,' he said. 'So, we're going to ask you to...'

He turned to see where Maggie was and saw that she was still on the passenger side of their patrol car, rooted to the spot, paying attention to the scruffy white van, which at that moment started its engine, sending out a plume of black exhaust fumes. He heard her shout 'Hey!' as she ran around to the driver's side of the van, then slammed the flat of her hand against the side as it started to pull away. As she reached the driver's door she grabbed the handle and threw it open.

'Stop!' she shouted. 'Cut the engine.'

Kevin was at a momentary loss, wondering whether he should go to her assistance or stay with the car driver. He saw his partner throwing herself into the van, across the driver's lap, and it glided to a halt on the gravelled and potholed lay-by as she switched off the ignition.

'Kevin! Over here quick!' she yelled as she stepped backwards from the van, rattling a bunch of keys which she had tugged from the ignition.

Kevin pointed to the car driver. 'But what about...' he began.

'This is more important. Get over here.'

Kevin abandoned the car and ran to assist his partner. When he got there, he saw the driver was thin-faced, hair close-cropped, probably in his late-thirties, and his short-sleeved shirt revealed scrawny arms covered in tattoos.

He had loser written all over him, and he spoke out of the side of his mouth like a hardened ex-convict.

'I haven't done nothing. What's all this in aid of?'

'Vehicle doesn't look roadworthy, if you ask me,' Maggie said.

'It's passed its MOT, back in March this year.'

Maggie's eyes travelled over the inside of the van. On top of the dashboard below the windscreen she spotted a leaflet. 'What's that?' she demanded.

'It's just an advertisement. Nothing important.'

Maggie held out her hand. 'Show me.'

Reluctantly, the scrawny van driver handed her the leaflet. She showed it to Kevin. 'What d'you make of that?'

Kevin pursed his lips as he scanned it. 'It's an advert for a boot sale at a caravan park in Brandon-on-Sea tomorrow.'

Maggie's eyes locked onto the driver's. 'You planning to attend this boot sale?'

'No. Haven't got nothing to sell, have I?'

'So, what are you doing with the leaflet?'

'It's just a leaflet, innit?'

'D'you mind getting out of the van, sir, and accompanying us to the rear, so we can see what you've got in the back.'

'It's empty. I'm not carrying nothing.'

Kevin drew himself up to his full height. 'Would you mind doing as my partner asked you, sir?'

Total defeat in the man's eyes as he slid in a snake-like movement from the van's cab and accompanied them towards the rear of his vehicle. As they neared the back, they saw the expensive car reverse onto the main road, and then with a squeal of tyres the car lurched forward, swerved crazily, righted itself, and screeched off along the road as if it was still being chased.

'He's only scarpered, the cheeky sod,' Kevin said.

'Never mind.' Maggie stared menacingly at the van driver. 'I think we might have landed the bigger fish. Let's get the back opened up, shall we?'

In the back of the van they found a treasure trove of tools and gardening implements, everything from hammers and saws to forks and spades, even the odd plastic paddling pool and garden recliner.

'Well, well, well,' Maggie said with a satisfied smile. 'You have been busy during the night. Planning on flogging this lot at the boot sale, were you? Right, let's get the cuffs on him.'

Kevin drove, and Maggie sat in the back of the patrol car with their prisoner. She asked him why he had parked in the lay-by, and he told her he was talking on his mobile when they pulled in behind him. But what she really wanted to know was why he hadn't headed out of the district as soon as possible after committing the burglaries, and their captive described, in a voice of gloomy resignation, how his van was in a state of disrepair and he was more likely to be stopped when there was less traffic on the road, and as there was the town carnival starting at midday, he thought he'd wait until later in the lay-by.

'Can't argue with that,' Kevin said cheerfully.

Maggie smiled. Both police constables were pleased with the result, and looked forward to the congratulations from their senior officers back at the police station.

Unfortunately, it wasn't quite the brilliant outcome they expected. The arrest of the burglar was almost disregarded because of the commotion taking place at the station. A far more serious incident had taken place. A woman with a toddler in a pushchair had been halfway across a zebra crossing when they were knocked down by a car. Both the mother and toddler were seriously injured and died in the ambulance on their way to hospital. The car responsible was a top of the range saloon car driven by a businessman, who was breathalysed and found to be over the permitted legal alcohol limit for driving. Even though he was devastated and shocked by his reckless act, he later protested that he was only a few milligrams over the limit, and the accident occurred because the mother had wheeled the pushchair so robustly onto the crossing giving him no time to react. But he received little sympathy from the arresting officers.

When Maggie received news of the fatality, she almost fainted from shock. And when the senior officers discovered the man had been in police custody for a short time, she and Kevin were questioned exhaustively. And while this went on, many of their colleagues speculated that they might be suspended. But when the story came out about the burglar, and the way he had been stopped from escaping, it soon became apparent the police officers were blameless for the incident and they were exonerated.

The tragedy and the reckless driving made headlines in the national press, especially when the number plate of the car was revealed. And then a reporter working for one of the tabloid nationals, jokingly said to a colleague, 'I could make a killing with this story.' He found his juicier story when he discovered the car was purchased by the businessman on June 6 just over two years prior to the accident. Which made it the sixth day of the sixth month, another two sixes to add to the six of the number plate. He got his sensational story and the rest of the media went berserk. The car was given a superstitious status, and it was thought to be jinxed. Headlines in the tabloid press screamed fearful speculation about the vehicle being a car from hell, driven by a devil.

None of which helped to assuage Maggie's feelings of guilt. She couldn't sleep at nights, and suffered from terrible depression which affected her work. She was absent on sick leave for a fortnight. She lived with her boyfriend, Terry, a plumber by trade, who worked for a successful company, was extremely busy and, although he was deeply sympathetic, he had very little time to spare, except late in the evening or on a Sunday, as he often had to work on a Saturday. During the time she spent absent from work, he heard her story so many times about wishing she had done things differently, and how if it hadn't been for her wanting to get a better arrest result, the mother and child would still be alive. And two weeks after the terrible accident, when the hack earned a centre page spread in his tabloid about the number plate and the car from hell, Terry used the superstition as an attempt to diminish Maggie's guilt, telling her she may have been the victim of strange circumstances beyond her control. But Maggie, who trained herself in pragmatic ways of thinking for her detective ambitions, was not superstitious and told Terry that she would gladly smash a mirror, because how could a broken mirror have any bearing on bringing her or them bad luck for seven years. The whole idea was ridiculous.

After she returned to work, she was occasionally struck by black moods. She was offered counselling, to which she responded favourably, and she came to accept the fact that neither she nor Kevin were in any way responsible for the drink driver's transgression any more than for any other criminal's felony.

She soon forgot about the incident and life returned to normal for her and Terry. Until the trial of the driver, when there were howls of derision from both public and press about his farcical three-year custodial sentence. The man was rich and could afford an excellent lawyer, who argued that his client was a responsible person, who only lived twenty miles from the hotel, and was sensible enough to stay the night rather than risk driving with alcohol in his blood. Then, almost a month after the businessman had been sentenced, the tabloid hack who wrote the original story about the errant car and discovered the number plate connection to the dates, found a way of wringing another salacious story from the accident. He interviewed the businessman's wife, who was suing her husband for divorce. Even before the accident, their marriage was rocky, and she accused him of having many messy affairs, and even their grown-up children no longer supported their father, and were horrified and sickened by his crime, and wanted little to do with him. As for the car, his wife was deeply superstitious, never walked under ladders or opened an umbrella indoors, and so she confined the car to their double garage, where it languished, abandoned and resented. But not before the hack photographed its final resting place, his camera focused on the number plate K1LL6.

When Maggie read this story in the Sunday tabloid, she was incensed. 'Listen to this,' she told Terry. 'This stupid woman has consigned a three-year-old top-of-the-range car to her garage and says it can rot as far as she is concerned. The reporter asked her if she intends selling it, and she says, "I wouldn't wish this car on anyone. It's bad luck. A killer. It's never going on any road ever again." What a stupid woman.'

Terry frowned deeply and stared at his Sunday roast. His silence about the car irritated Maggie.

'What's wrong?' she demanded.

'Well, she might have a point. I mean, it's her husband's car, and he also had a five-year ban on driving, so I guess it would be better all round to keep the car off the road.'

'Better for who?'

'Well, you know – there might be a jinx on it.'

Maggie snorted disparagingly. 'Because of the number plate? That's bloody ridiculous. It's like all these superstitious morons, believing in nonsense. Things which don't exist. Where's the proof that number plate had anything to do with those deaths? It was the bloke who'd had a skinful the night before. That's all it was. And just because some reporter wants to make a name for himself—'

A subtle smile tugged at Terry's mouth as he thought of a way to challenge his girlfriend. 'What if it was your car, Maggs? Would you be quite happy to drive it knowing…?'

'Of course I would,' she interrupted. 'Wouldn't bother me at all. Great car like that. I've taken an advanced driving test, and I wouldn't be so stupid as to drive under the influence. Expensive, luxury car like that would be a joy to drive.'

Terry's smile widened. 'If that's how you feel, why not get in touch with the wife, and make her an offer for the car. You might get a bargain.'

'Don't be silly, Terry. She said in the paper that it's never going on the road again.'

'Car like that must be thirty or forty grand at least. Offer her two-thousand cash, I bet she'd take it.'

'You're forgetting something. The car belongs to her husband, and he's inside.'

'He can sign the papers over to her. I mean, what use is the car to him? In five years' time it will rot if nobody drives it. Or is it because you're scared – just as superstitious as the rest of them?'

'Terry!' Maggie snapped, anger in her eyes. 'I wish I could prove to you—' And she stopped as the anger gave way to a sudden thought. 'Maybe I can. Maybe I can find a way to persuade this stupid woman to give up the car.'

Knowing his girlfriend had taken the bait, Terry grinned. 'Let's hope so. Be great to own a car like that. And just to be on the safe side, we can change the registration.'

'Change the registration?' Maggie questioned, shaking her head vehemently. 'Over my dead body!'

Terry stopped smiling as he felt a cold shadow on his back, hovering like an angel of death.

***

The house was massive, with a long drive through ornate wrought iron gates leading up to an enormous front door sandwiched by plantation-style pillars. Although Maggie knew very little about architecture, she recognised the style from similar houses she had seen in films like *Twelve Years a Slave*. She parked her Astra in front of the pillars, walked up to the front door and rang the bell. From the size and opulence of the house, she almost expected the door to be answered by a maid. But it was his wife who answered the door, Maggie recognised her from the newspaper photograph.

'Mrs Glynford?'

The woman frowned. 'Yes?'

'I'm the police officer who failed to arrest your husband on the day he killed that woman and toddler.'

The frown deepened, and there was a pause before the woman replied, as if recovering from shocking news. 'Well, that's hardly your fault, is it? It was my husband who'd been drinking. We had screaming rows about it. So, what is it you want?'

'I want to buy your husband's car.'

The woman laughed nervously. 'Read about it in the paper, did you? How I have no intention of selling. Bloody car is jinxed.'

'If I can prove to you that the car had nothing to do with...'

Like flicking a hand at an irritating insect, the woman waved it aside, 'Why don't you come in and we can talk about it.'

Surprised at the sudden change, Maggie stepped inside as the woman closed the door.

'Why don't we go into the lounge?'

As Maggie followed, she noticed the large hall was stacked with enormous cardboard boxes, with the name of a local removal firm printed on them. 'Are you leaving the district?' she asked as they entered the living room, which she noticed was real stockbroker chintzy, rather fussy for her taste. She sat in a comfortable winged armchair, and the woman sat opposite, leaning forward on the edge of her seat as if she was in a hurry to get this conversation over with.

'Yes, I'm leaving. Going back to where I came from. But even that hundred odd miles is not far enough away from the memories of living with that bastard.'

'And I'm guessing you won't be taking your husband's car, so you'll need someone to take it off your hands.'

'You guessed right. I can hardly leave it in the garage.'

Maggie's heart thumped excitedly, knowing she was close to a result. She and Terry could probably afford two- or three-thousand for it, but knew she had to start negotiating at the lowest amount. 'Of course,' she began tentatively, 'when I read in the paper the car was being abandoned, I thought it was such a shame. But my boyfriend and me... well, we don't have more to offer than a thousand for it. I know it's worth thousands more, but in the circumstances...'

The woman waved it aside, almost with a show of aggression. 'Don't bullshit a bull-shitter,' she said. 'You can change the registration of the car, and the jinx might disappear along with that number plate.'

Knowing how superstitious the woman was, Maggie didn't admit she had no intention of changing the registration. 'I will change the number plate,' she lied. 'But there's always a chance the car will still be jinxed.'

The woman screwed up her face with worry. 'Oh my God!'

'But I've taken the police advanced motoring test. I assure you if anyone's capable of driving that car—'

'I just don't want another accident in that car on my conscience.'

'I assure you, Mrs Glynford, everything will be fine.'

There was a pause while the woman deliberated. 'Oh, well, if you're sure. And if I can get my husband to sign the car over to me, shall we say five thousand?'

'Way over what we can afford, I'm afraid. Like I said, when we read in the paper...'

'If you can go to three-thousand – cash – that car's yours. It will serve that bastard right. He won't know he's getting sod all for it. I'll tell him it's been crushed. Which is really what should happen to it. It ought to be punished, crushed into pulp, for killing that mother and child.'

Stupid, superstitious bitch!' Maggie thought unkindly. *It's her husband who should be pulped.* She stood up, trying to keep the excitement out of her voice. 'Thank you, Mrs Glynford – three-thousand cash it is.' She took out a notebook, wrote down her name and phone number, tore out the sheet and handed it to the woman. 'Let me know as soon as the car's transferred in your name and I'll be over with the cash.'

'If my husband agrees – and I can't see any reason he won't – it's got to happen within the next two weeks.'

'I take it, that's when you're moving.'

'Right. And I'll be glad to see the back of this area. Nothing but bad memories. Especially now Roger's a murdering drunk driver.'

***

While they waited for the phone call telling them Mrs Glynford's husband had signed over the car to his wife, Maggie and Terry talked excitedly every day about their lucky bargain. Terry, although he claimed he wasn't superstitious, argued that it was like the difference between being an atheist and an agnostic. While an atheist might challenge a religious person to prove there was a God, neither could an atheist prove that God didn't exist. Whereas an agnostic could keep an open mind. And so, Terry argued, it was better to be safe than sorry and change the registration of the car.

Reluctantly, Maggie agreed, although a secret part of her was relieved she no longer had to suffer the niggling fear of that ghastly number plate buried in a remote corner of her mind.

Mrs Glynford called nine days after Maggie's visit, telling her everything was now arranged and that she should pick up the car as soon as possible. As it was less than ten miles, and Terry was working on a central heating project on a new housing estate, she arranged to go over by taxi. On the journey over, the taxi driver was chatty, but Maggie was lost in her own reveries, already imagining herself behind the wheel of that superior automobile, and she answered monosyllabically. As they got into the long stretch of road locals called the Six Mile Spread, with fields and hedgerows on one side, and on the other a sheer drop into the gravel pits a hundred feet below the highway, she heard the taxi driver say something about an accident waiting to happen. She nodded agreement from the back seat, and muttered something vague about being careful and not taking ridiculous chances by overtaking on this stretch of road.

After she was dropped off, she did the deal with Mrs Glynford, and was led to the garage to take possession of her car. But however extravagantly sleek and beautiful the car was, even Maggie felt a slight vibration of dread as she read K1LL6 on the number plate. She shook the moment's apprehension away, telling herself she would one day be a detective, and detectives do not believe in psychic phenomena to explain mysteries.

She shook hands with Mrs Glynford, wished her luck with her relocation, then eased the car out of the drive. As she stopped by the gates, waiting to turn into the road, she thought the engine had stalled it was so silent. She smiled contentedly. This was motoring. Such a smooth drive and such power under the bonnet. It was early in the afternoon, not much traffic about, and she drove steadily, slowly at first, enjoying the feel of the car and the luxurious smell of the leather upholstery. And then a black thought darkened her mood. This car, her and Terry's gain, had come about because of the death of a mother and child, and for a moment she felt guilty for taking advantage of someone else's misfortune. But then, as she got to a T-junction and turned left onto the main road heading towards Six Mile Spread, she forgot about the circumstances of her good fortune, and relaxed. It was such an easy car to drive. There was nothing on the road. A long straight stretch, and already her speedometer needle was touching sixty without her realising. She chuckled. The car could cruise effortlessly, and she must have covered two of the six miles already, with the fields on her right, and the long drop into gravel pits on her left. But the car was perfection, fantastic engineering, and was steady and solid. She could steer with her little finger and it would keep going along the Six Mile Spread and wouldn't swing a fraction from its very straight course.

But because of the straight road, and the millpond ease of the drive, she saw the needle had crept up to seventy-five. She was about to ease her foot off the accelerator, when she saw a car coming from the opposite direction. She had been distracted for less than a second, but suddenly there was an almighty bang, and she felt the steering wheel wobble and the car bounced uncontrollably as it veered into the right-hand side of the road. Her mouth opened in a silent scream as she prepared for the head-on collision with the other car. She braced herself for the crash, but to avoid the collision, the other car wheeled sharply to its right side. She heard the skid and the squeal of breaks of the other car as her own car rumbled and bumped across a shallow ditch and into a ploughed field.

Maggie unclipped her seatbelt, opened the door and ran across the road to see what had happened to the other car. It was nowhere to be seen, having smashed through the wooden fence and gone over the edge into the gravel pit. She peered through the gap in the fence and to her horror saw the car was a fireball, a burning wreck. No one could possibly have survived the crash. She fell to her knees, screaming and crying.

After the accident was investigated, it was discovered that Maggie's new car had hit a thin strip of metal in the road, creating friction which punctured the offside front tyre. It was not considered a human error and Maggie was absolved of any fault.

The car which crashed into the gravel pit killed the driver and three passengers: a husband, his wife and their two young children.

Following this accident, the press became hysterical again, expressing the opinion that the number plate had attained its target of killing six people. The frenzied reporting of the tragedy lasted for over a week, until another bigger news item overshadowed it. Maggie, too upset to work, was given leave of absence. As for the car, Terry drove it (carefully) to a breaker's yard, where it was weighed for scrap, for which he received the sum of a hundred and ten pounds.

Jimmy Hands, who worked at the breaker's yard couldn't bear to see a beautiful car like that end up in the crusher, so he offered his boss five-hundred for it, plus the money paid out for the scrap value. Jimmy then relicensed the vehicle and bought another number plate. He was also shrewd enough to sell the old plate for an undisclosed sum to a museum.

The New Scotland Yard Black Museum is not open to the public, but if you are fortunate enough to be invited to visit this strange and sometimes rather macabre museum, displaying exhibits of crime, don't be surprised if you see a car number plate K1LL6.

8: The Man on the Train

When multiple rapist Tony Pelchatt was paroled after serving only eight years in prison, there was an outcry from the public. Understandably, I thought. The uproar was fuelled by the media coverage of his release. And the moral indignation of the press, including my own, went on for weeks, demanding answers from the parole board, who claimed that this man who had savagely raped at least forty young women at knife point was no longer a danger to the public. What drove the social media into a frenzy over Pelchatt's early release was the reluctance of the parole board to offer any explanation for their decision. Why, the social media raged, did they no longer consider this man a danger and a threat? And still the parole board claimed their reasons were strictly confidential.

My editor wanted me to find a different angle to the story. I racked my brains for another way of presenting it, but the media had milked the story for all it was worth, and I argued that by trying to add more fury to the fire of hatred burning inside everyone, we might end up with a damp squib and bore our readers. But if you knew my editor, you would realise that it is pointless trying to argue with him. He was determined we should look for another slant on the story, suggesting I try to discover what Pelchatt did in the year-long gap after the last rape on Abinger Common before he was apprehended. But even this was old news, and it was thought the man discontinued his abominable crimes simply because he feared getting caught. My editor also suggested I try to find the parole board's motive in their foolhardy and lenient judgement in releasing a serial rapist way ahead of serving his life sentence. But I had already been down this route, along with dozens of other reporters, and the parole board's collective mouth remained firmly shut, and there was no possibility of a leak.

And then, within hours of the editor's pep talk with me, the big story landed metaphorically on my desk, without my having to do any legwork. Because of my byline and balanced coverage of the serial rapist story, a man called our paper and asked to speak to me personally. When I spoke to the young man – at least, he sounded young on the telephone – he said he knew the reason the parole board brought forward Pelchatt's release, even though he was dead against it. I was intrigued. How could he possibly know of the parole board's decision? When I pressed him for an answer, he said he was reluctant to go into details over the phone, and asked if we could meet somewhere private, as the information he had was confidential. We sometimes get crank calls, and I almost dismissed this as one of them, but there was something about his businesslike manner that made me want to meet him. We arranged to meet later that afternoon in the lounge of a London hotel. He said his name was Graham Ewens. I Googled him before I left and found a doctor of that name living in Kingston-on-Thames. And then I recalled that most of Pelchatt's rapes had been in rural parts of Surrey, Sussex and Berkshire.

The taxi dropped me off at 4.30 and I hoped I wouldn't have long to wait for my contact, who described himself as dark-haired, in his mid-thirties, and would be wearing a light blue, two-piece suit, and a multi-coloured tie with horizontal stripes.

Fortunately, as it was early November, the hotel was not as busy as I expected, and I was pleased to see my contact had arrived early. He was seated behind a small round table in the lounge.

'Mr Ewens?' I said and introduced myself. He stood up and we shook hands. He was well over six feet tall, broad shouldered, quite good looking in a rugged way, with dark brown eyes and a slightly crooked nose that looked as if it might have been broken. As I sat in the chair opposite him, I said, 'Or is it Doctor Ewens?'

He smiled as he settled back in his chair. 'Presumably you Googled me.'

'I'm sorry,' I said. 'It's usual in these situations. And I wanted to see if you were related to anyone on the parole board.'

He shrugged. 'I don't know anyone on the parole board. If you think this is just a question of an angry citizen exposing their reasons for releasing that monster, think again. This is a much bigger story, I promise. So big, in fact, that I will need to impose certain conditions. But first let me show you a document.'

He reached down by his chair, rummaged in a holdall, took a sheaf of papers from it, and handed them to me. A waitress came over and asked if we wanted drinks. Doctor Ewens asked for a bottle of lager and I ordered the same.

After our drinks had been served, and I had read the first page of the document, I said, 'This is a subpoena from Pelchatt's solicitors. He's suing you. Taking you to court. What the hell for?'

He sipped his lager slowly before speaking. 'Before I give you the full story – an exclusive – I would like to know that in the event of him winning the case, your newspaper will pay me a substantial amount to cover any damages or costs.'

'It would have to be a hell of a good story.'

'Believe me, it is.'

'And I would need to speak to my editor first. But suppose he doesn't like the story.'

'Then we don't have a deal. But if you publish it—'

'Then you get your money.'

'In the event of my losing the court case.'

To say I was intrigued would be putting it mildly. I grabbed my iPhone, excused myself and went out into the street to call the editor. I was surprised at how readily he agreed; he figured a civil action by scum like Pelchatt must surely lose any sympathy from a judge. I explained that we didn't know what the action was about, but my editor laughed dismissively, saying he had a good feeling about this story, and we ought to go for it.

And go for it I did. I switched the Dictaphone on, placed it on the table in front of Doctor Ewens and listened to the start of his compelling tale.

***

He spotted her when she got on the Horsham train at Epsom. He must have guessed – hoping, maybe – she might get off at one of the smaller stations between there and Horsham. She happened to catch his eye as the train left Epsom and he smiled, nothing overdone, just a tentative communication between two fellow passengers. And then he looked away, the smile merely a good citizen gesture, then buried his head in a copy of *The Times*.

She was aware of his presence and could feel his piercing glances at her over the top of his paper from time to time. It was late on Monday afternoon the last week in August, just a week before the schools started the new term, so there was not the usual rowdy crowd of schoolkids on board. There were only two other passengers in the carriage. Later in the journey, as the train pulled out of Dorking station, she took out her mobile to make a call. She gasped loudly.

'Oh, no!' she exclaimed. 'Bloody battery's gone.'

He lowered his paper, suddenly alert. 'Problem?' he said.

'Yes, I forgot to charge my phone. And I want my parents to pick me up at

Ockley station. They're off on a cruise on Thursday, and I need to spend time with them before they go.'

He chuckled warmly. 'No such thing as problems, only solutions.' He held out his mobile phone. 'Why don't you borrow mine?'

'Are you sure?'

'I'd like to help,' he smiled. 'It's only one phone call, after all. Not like you're calling Australia.'

She took the phone from him. 'No, it's just outside Capel village. Thank you.'

'You're welcome.'

He politely pretended to read while she made the call, although she could tell he was listening intently.

'Hello, Mummy? My train arrives at Ockley in less than ten. Can you or Dad pick me up? I know it's not that far, but I need to spend time with you before you go. After all, I'll be all alone in the house. No, no. I didn't mean it like that. I just meant I'll be a bit lonely, that's all. But I start at sixth form college next week, so I'll have a lot to think about. OK. I must go. See you at the station soon, yeah? Ciao!'

Smiling, she handed him back his phone. 'Thank you.'

'You're very welcome. I hope you get home OK.'

'Yes, Mum or Dad'll meet me at Ockley.'

'I don't want to be rude, but I couldn't help overhearing your conversation. Your parents are off on a cruise. Anywhere nice?'

'Yes. They fly to Italy on Thursday and they're cruising the Mediterranean.'

'Very nice too.'

They made polite conversation for the next ten minutes, until the train pulled into Ockley station. Then she thanked him once more, waved goodbye as the doors opened, and stepped down from the train. As it pulled away, she noticed he was now deeply engrossed in his paper and didn't bother to look in her direction.

***

I interrupted his story at this point. 'Presumably, that was him. Pelchatt.'

He nodded, and I noticed the tension in his face, the way his jaw tightened, and his fists clenched.

'But who was the girl?' I asked him. 'Was she your girlfriend?'

'My sister.'

'How old? Fifteen? Sixteen?'

'Sixteen.'

'And you were how old?'

'I was in my early twenties. I was at university. Studying medicine, in my second year.'

'This chance meeting on the train, between your sister and Pelchatt. Bad luck her phone battery went flat, because now he had your family phone number on his mobile.'

He stared at me, his expression impossible to interpret. I felt a gnawing in my stomach, anticipating a tragedy about to raise its dreadful head, and I wondered if his sister was another of Pelchatt's victims.

'Oh, he had our phone number all right. Of course, at this stage we had no idea – just a suspicion – that it was the serial rapist.'

'Why would you even be suspicious?'

'Because of all the rapes within a geographical pattern. We reckoned the rapist lived anywhere between Horsham and Epsom.'

'But if the police couldn't work that one out—'

He sighed impatiently. 'Look, a friend of mine at the same university studied criminology. He was the one who worked it out. He knows about profiling and how the police don't really trust it. Had they realised in the Yorkshire Ripper case that Sutcliffe changed his address halfway through the years of those horrific murders, and the area of the crimes changed accordingly, they might have caught him sooner. The police attitude to profiling is sometimes like the way many of us in the medical profession regard homeopathy.'

I was aware we had digressed from the main story. 'I'm sorry, Graham, I shouldn't have interrupted you. I'll let you tell it in your own words, and I'll only interrupt if I need clarification for something. OK?'

He nodded, and his mouth tightened grimly. Aware he was getting jittery, he paused and tried to relax. Then continued with his story.

**

Of course, we had no way of knowing if the man on the train was Pelchatt. But the police investigation was a failure, a total disaster. Something had to be done about this monster. It was time to protect our young women, and I felt it my duty to cut this cancer from society. I not only wanted to catch the rapist, I wanted to shut him down for good.

When my sister, Nicola, pretended her phone battery was flat on that Monday, and Pelchatt offered to help, she dialled our landline on his mobile. But it was a fake call. She spoke to our answering machine. Her conversation with our parents was a pretence. It was on the previous Saturday they left for their Mediterranean cruise. And it wasn't true that Nicola was alone in the house; I would be with her for another two weeks until I went back to university. But we still had no way of knowing if the man on the train was Pelchatt? Not until the phone rang on Wednesday morning. When I answered it, the caller claimed to be delivering a parcel and was lost and asked if we were at such and such an address. No, I told him, we were… and I gave him our address. He thanked me and hung up quickly, probably congratulating himself on how easily he obtained our address.

The trap was set.

If the man on the train was the rapist, we guessed he would make his move on Friday, knowing Nicola was alone then.

But what if we were wrong?

Was the man on the train a helpful citizen, and the phone call on Wednesday morning merely a coincidence?

We had no way of knowing.

But we were prepared. Just in case.

Because it was late summer, it started to get dark around 8.45. Nine o'clock came and went, and the sun had set. By nine-thirty it was pitch black outside. If the man on the train was Pelchatt, the rapist, then he might come on another night. And a terrible thought occurred to me. What if he planned to leave it for a few weeks? I would be back at university and Nicola really would be all alone in the house. I began to have terrible doubts about my vigilante behaviour and…

It was just past nine-thirty when the doorbell rang. It had to be him. As arranged, Nicola answered the door. Fortunately, there was no glass in our front door, it was solid, and I crept to a position behind it, ready to protect her when she opened it, the rag soaked in chloroform in my left hand.

Adopting a puzzled, who-can-it-be-at-this-time-of-night expression, she eased open the door. There was a long pause. And then he spoke in a menacing tone. "Remember me?" he said. "From the train on Monday?" I heard him laugh. I was close behind the door and I saw Nicola step back into the hall, with a choking cry of terror. I saw his left-hand reach around the door as he stepped inside and slammed it shut. He had a knife in his right hand, and he saw me out of the corner of his eye. He started to turn towards me, bringing the knife arcing around as I slammed my right fist into the side of his head. I'm quite strong, I used to play rugby regularly, and he dropped like a heavy sack onto his knees. I smothered his face with the rag, felt him go limp, and let him fall forward on to the carpet.

For a moment, Nicola and I exchanged looks, hardly believing we had him. Straight into our trap. Caught like a fly in our web. That was when I saw doubt clouding my sister's expression, a mixture of regret and fear. "I think we should call the police," she said. But I was determined this man would never rape another woman. "Even if he gets a life sentence," I argued. "This bastard looks like he's in his early thirties. And a life sentence doesn't necessarily mean literally life. No, we've talked about this. There's only one way of making certain he never rapes anyone ever again."

I saw my sister shiver, and I told her to go upstairs to her room, saying I would deal with it from here on. Scurrying like a frightened animal, Nicola hurried upstairs, and after I heard the slam of her bedroom door, I leant over Pelchatt, grabbed him under the arms and dragged him into the dining room.

I was already prepared. The dining room table covered with a rubber sheet, and the surgical instruments on an occasional table nearby. I found undressing Pelchatt revolting, knowing of his detestable history, but I had no regrets for what I was about to do.

I struggled to get him on to the table but, like I said, I'm quite strong, and I managed it without much difficulty. I strapped him down with leather belts, over his legs and torso, pinning his arms to the table. I poured myself a large whisky and waited for him to come around.

At first, he blinked several times, and I could see he was disorientated. And then, as he tried to move, I could see his recent memory shifting into focus. He tried to speak but his lips were dry. "Listen to me," I said. "Your abominable crimes are over. You will never rape another woman. Not after I've operated on you." I picked up a scalpel and waved it in front of his face, and he knew right away what was about to happen. "No. Please," he begged. "Anything but that. Please. I might bleed to death." I laughed without a shred of warmth or humanity, hoping he would suffer as much as his forty victims. "No chance of that," I said. "I'm a medical student, training to be a doctor. It will be a neat operation. And just so we don't wake the neighbourhood, I think I'd better gag you." As if switched on by a tap, tears ran from his eyes as he cried, "At least put me under. Please." Shaking my head as I reached for the handkerchief and gaffer tape to gag him, I said, "Those women you raped were aware of what was happening. The pain you caused them. And you're going to suffer in the same way."

I gagged him. I heard his muffled cries and groans through it. Then I put on the surgical gloves, picked up the scalpel and began to slice through his penis.

**

As I stared at Doctor Ewens, I imagined the scene in his family dining room, the rapist strapped helplessly to the table. I held my breath in the last moments of his narrative, and now I let it out slowly, deflating like a slow puncture.

He stared at me, waiting for my response. The inevitable question he knew I would ask.

'What did you do with—?'

I couldn't bring myself to say it.

He smiled calmly, seemed relieved his story was almost over. 'You mean what did I do with the offending penis?' He shrugged. 'No doubt our hungry wildlife devoured it. Foxes aren't choosy about their food.'

After a thoughtful pause, I said, 'That's why there were no rapes for a year before he was caught. And presumably, when he was arrested for violence in a pub brawl, it was because of his sexual frustration.'

Ewens nodded. 'Exactly. And when they took his DNA they had a match to one of his victims.'

'Because of the – um – operation you performed, do you think that was why the parole board reduced his sentence?'

The doctor pursed his lips thoughtfully before answering. 'It could be. Because they knew he wasn't capable of raping anyone. I still think that monster should have served his full life sentence.'

'So do I. And my newspaper story will reflect that opinion.'

'Thank you. And I want this story, and all the exposure it engenders, to be old news by the time I'm the defendant in the civil trial. I almost think Pelchatt is hoping the story of his castration will be a shocking surprise in the courtroom.'

'What about your parents? Won't they be horrified when they find out about—'

'They already know,' he cut in. 'I had to tell them before this becomes public. They were horrified, of course. My father took it better than my mother. I think she worries about my GP practice and how that will affect my patients in future.'

'And what about your sister?'

'She studied languages. She married a Frenchman, lives in Paris and works as in interpreter. I know she was an accomplice in the way she set him up, but all along she thought I was just going to detain him until the police arrived. And no one can prove differently.'

'But it will still come as a shock when the story hits the streets day after tomorrow.'

He glanced at his watch. 'That's why I'm booked on Eurostar from St

Pancras at eight tonight. I want to tell her and my brother-in-law in person.'

We exchanged business cards, and I asked him to call me day or night if he thought of anything else to add to the story. We shook hands and I wished him luck with his sister in Paris. Then I jumped in a cab and headed back to the office. I couldn't wait to see the look on my editor's face when I gave him an account of the story. One which had fallen into my lap like manna.

***

My story made not waves but a great tsunami. It was discussed from every viewpoint on radio and television, and it rocked social media with many tweets saying it served the perpetrator of the rapes right, and others decrying vigilante behaviour and making a mockery of the law. But at least Doctor Ewens got the public mostly on his side.

And then came his civil trial, which he and his defence team cleverly decided to opt for a minimal defence and get it over with quickly. One newspaper headlined the trial as The Good Doctor Versus the Eunuch, while the tabloids went for more obvious punning captions. The trial lasted only two days, and Pelchatt won the case. There were howls of indignation from the media. This was soon quietened by the judge's award for damages. Pelchatt was to receive only one-pound compensation for his loss.

My paper paid for the court costs, and my editor considered it well worth it for the size of the story. Humongous, he called it. Humongous.

And it didn't end there. Doctor Ewens faced a criminal charge for violent behaviour and grievous bodily harm. He was sentenced to two years – suspended.

I wondered how this affected him as a GP in Kingston-on-Thames, and I discovered his practice was more popular than ever.

As for Pelchatt, he committed suicide. Unable to live with the humiliation of his castration at the hands of the good doctor, he threw himself under a train.

End of story. And the next scoop will be another man-made tragedy. It's how we sell newspapers.

9: A Cautionary Tale for Ill-Mannered Children

Old Charlie Griffits wheezed up the Town Hall steps, wishing he'd given up smoking more than a decade ago. Now in his late eighties, he knew giving up smoking at the age of seventy-eight was merely pandering to the admonishments of his doctor, and he desperately craved a return to the sanity of nicotine.

It was three in the afternoon, and there were two queues at the enquiries counter. Charlie stopped just inside the door, surveying the municipal hall, wondering which queue to join. Both were for enquiries, so there was no telling which queue he should join. He saw a young mother, at the head of one queue of four women, her baby in its buggy, grizzling through its dummy-stoppered mouth. There appeared to be an argument going on between the receptionist and the young mum as she reluctantly parted with some ten-pound notes. Perhaps her council rent was short of what was owed. Charlie decided to join the other queue, consisting of three men and only one woman. Men deal with things quicker, Charlie reckoned. Like getting on the bus. They always have money ready, whereas the women wait until they're on the bus before rooting through handbags and purses for the right money. And Charlie's fuse these days was getting shorter and shorter.

Twenty minutes later, his feet aching, and gout throbbing in his ankles, he confronted his receptionist – a pudding-faced youngster with disinterested eyes. 'Yes?' she enquired expressionlessly, which niggled Charlie from the off. He could hear himself telling his deceased wife how he gave the receptionist a blazing sermon, made her see the error of her ways, and left her gasping and contrite. Charlie often had these conversations with his dead wife in their back garden.

'Yes?' the receptionist repeated, undisguised impatience in her tone.

Charlie drew himself up to his full height, although his back ached. 'I have come to the Town Hall to lodge a complaint,' he boomed.

'What seems to be the problem?'

Charlie smacked his lips together. When he spoke, he enunciated every word, using the tone he reserved for simpletons and disinterested civil servants. 'The problem lies with the 281 buses. Which I catch twice a week. And the children crowding on to it at 4.30 pm when they are let out of school. Have these children no manners?'

The receptionist blinked rapidly and waited for Charlie to continue.

'What do their teachers and parents teach them these days? Not manners, that's for sure. Youngsters sitting in priority seats – seats reserved for the elderly – and still they don't offer to stand to let someone like myself sit down. I'm eighty-seven you know. And I sometimes see elderly women standing, with young brats sitting comfortably, simply because they got on a stop earlier than us pensioners who have been to the shops.'

Charlie ran out of steam, smacked his lips again, and waited for the receptionist's response.

'Well, what do you want us to do about it?'

Irritated by her lack of interest, he tapped a finger on the counter for emphasis. 'I want you to instruct the bus company to tell their drivers to demand that the seats – all the seats – be reserved for adults. Children are young enough to stand.'

The receptionist shook her head. 'We can't do that?'

'Oh? And why not?'

'Because there is no rule about children who have purchased a bus ticket not being allowed to sit down.'

'But don't you see,' Charlie said, glaring at her, 'it's a question of good manners.'

'Yes, I agree with you there.'

Charlie nodded and smiled with self-satisfaction. At least now they were getting somewhere.

'But,' the receptionist continued, 'there is nothing we can do about this. The children's behaviour is up to their parents. Not the bus company. Or the town council.'

'You're wrong,' Charlie snapped. 'Wrong, wrong, wrong. I would like to see someone about this – no disrespect to present company, of course – but I would like to discuss this with someone in greater authority.'

Glad of an excuse to get away from the dreary queue, even if only for a few minutes' respite, the receptionist said, 'You can have a word with my supervisor if you like. I'll go and see if she's prepared to have a word with you. If you don't mind waiting for another ten or fifteen minutes. She's a bit busy right now. I'll call you when she's available. Could I have your name, please?'

'Charles Griffits.'

'Would you like to take a seat over there, Mr Griffiths?'

'No, not Griffiths. Griffits. We all dropped our aitches in our family, see.'

The receptionist looked blank.

'It was a joke. There's no letter H in Griffits.'

The receptionist's mouth opened in confusion. 'I'll just have a word with my supervisor,' she said as she walked away.

'Thick as two short planks,' Charlie mumbled. Then reluctantly, because he didn't like to be kept waiting, he shuffled over to a large, cushioned bench seat. After five minutes of gnashing his teeth impatiently, and becoming more irriated, he stood up suddenly and hurried, puffing and wheezing, away from the Town Hall, to the bus stop. It was time to deal with the ill-mannered school children. *The council's defeatist attitude is shameful, Rosie*, he explained to his dead wife. In his head, not aloud. Because there were others at the stop waiting to board the next bus, and he wouldn't want anyone to think he was going a bit senile.

When the bus came, he saw it was full of schoolkids, all seated luxuriously while many adults stood. Charlie boarded the bus, glowered at the driver as though he was to blame for the seated children, and pressed his bus pass on to the template. He took his ticket and elbowed his way past some older children, shoving them roughly aside, and moved towards the priority seats. When he saw two young boys seated there, he was about to rant and rave when one of the boys, an 11-year-old, vacated the seat and mumbled, 'Would you like a seat?'

'Thank you, son,' Charlie said, and sat next to the other boy. He turned to him and said, 'At least your friend has got manners. It'll save his life one day. You see if it won't.'

Charlie, although placated by the mannerly gesture, looked around at the rest of the passengers. There were school children seated, and at least half a dozen adults standing. Admittedly not elderly, but it wasn't right that adults should be standing while little brats sat in relative comfort. He was about to start yelling, mouthing off about their bad manners, when the bus pulled into the stop outside Sainsbury's. All the adults alighted, along with some of the children, but other children waiting for the bus outside the supermarket clambered aboard, so that the bus was just as crowded, but now Charlie was the only adult on board. And then, a great coincidence. An opportunity to teach these young louts some manners.

It occasionally happened that bus drivers needed to relieve themselves and used the toilets in Sainsbury's. Charlie could see this driver desperately needed to go. And once he had disappeared into the supermarket, Charlie stood up and grabbed the little boy with good manners. 'This is where you get off, son,' he said.

'But I'm going all the way to the village,' the boy protested.

'No, you're not, son. You'll thank me for this. There'll be another bus along in about fifteen minutes. Catch that one.'

Scared, the youngster scuttled on to the pavement as Charlie opened the driver's cab door and sat behind the wheel. Having observed the way drivers shut the doors, he operated the switch and the doors clattered shut. He heard some of his young passengers crying out in alarm and asking what was happening, but he ignored them and switched on the ignition. He had driven vans for a living before he retired, so driving one of these compact little buses was no problem.

Pulling away from the Sainsbury's stop he spotted the driver coming out of the supermarket. Seeing the startled look on his face, Charlie laughed gleefully. Now some of the children began crying and screaming as he weaved his way through the traffic, almost crashing into a lorry on the other side of the road. He put his foot down, laughing manically as he saw the needle hitting sixty, and this was in a built-up area. Children screamed. Some buried head in hands and sobbed, knowing their lives were now in the hands of a dangerous lunatic.

The bus weaved crazily from side to side, and went through a red light, cars from the other directions screeching to a skidding halt. And still the bus picked up speed, heading for the road out of town.

'Where are we going? Where's he taking us?' one of the older children shouted.

Charlie heard him and answered, 'To purgatory. To teach you all a lesson in manners.'

None of the children knew the road they hurtled along. High walls on either side flashed by as the bus drove at reckless speed. This triggered a blood-curdling scream of fear, nothing like the indulgent roller-coaster cry of adventurous children. The bus hurtled towards two solid doors. And just as the youngsters thought a crash was inevitable, the doors opened, and the bus vanished into a dark tunnel. With an almighty clang the doors shut behind them and the wheels squealed as Charlie applied the brakes.

All that could be heard in the pitch black was the collective sobbing of children. 'Where are we?' one of the older teenagers asked, a tremor in his voice.

Charlie laughed demonically. 'Welcome to purgatory,' he said.

A light glowed at the end of the tunnel, and Charlie drove slowly towards it. The tunnel dipped steeply as the bus descended, and as they got nearer to the circular aperture at the end of the tunnel, the light became more fantastic, shimmering in extraordinary colours like the Aurora Borealis. Charlie eased the bus through the camera-like aperture and into an enormous underground cavern. He stopped the bus and surveyed his surroundings with familiarity, as if he had been here many times before. The children, silent now and awed by the enormity of the cavern, stared through the windows at the dreadful hallucinatory image of the grotesque cavern. It was so vast that the dark roof could barely be seen. The landscape within the cavern was hilly, with enormous wheels on some of the hills with ladders leading up to them. Some of the wheels turned slowly, creaking and clanking as cogs slotted into place, and rickety-looking bridges joined several hills. Blotted like haphazard holes at the side of some of the higher hills were dark forbidding caves, out of which weaved slimy tentacles belonging to unearthly creatures. There were also empty egg-shaped cages, scattered around some of the lower hills, and heavy metal balls at the bottom of steep slopes. From beyond the hills came the sounds of tormented souls, and the wail of strange creatures, the noise of ravenous monsters anticipating a banquet of raw human meat.

'Everyone off the bus,' Charlie demanded cheerfully as he opened the doors.

'I want to go home,' a twelve-year-old girl cried. 'I want my mummy.'

'Turn this bus around and let's go back,' a teenage boy suggested.

'This bus goes nowhere,' Charlie replied. 'It's set to explode in five minutes, and you'll all be blown to smithereens if you don't get off.'

There was a mad scramble as all the children rushed along the aisles and fought each other to get through the doors. As soon as the bus had emptied, Charlie climbed out. The children grouped together, shivering and miserable, although it was hot and humid in the vast underground chamber. Numb with terror, in a state of deep shock, the children were like frozen zombies, and the weaving multi-coloured lights threw disturbing patterns across their frightened faces.

Suddenly, a squelching sound, like someone walking through treacle. They all turned and saw a thin man in a floppy hat approaching. 'Ah! Mr Bosch,' Charlie greeted him. 'I'm glad we made it. These children need a lesson in manners.'

'I will make the punishment fit the crime,' Bosch said, and addressed the smallest, youngest girl. 'And what is your crime, little girl?'

The girl pouted sulkily. 'Nothing. This man' – she pointed rudely at Charlie – 'thinks we ought to stand up to give adults a seat on the bus. But I paid for my ticket. Why shouldn't I sit down?'

'You see,' Charlie told Bosch, 'no humility or remorse. What will be the most fitting punishment?'

Bosch gestured to one of the hills. 'She will climb that ladder and operate the wheel. Round and round until she is genuinely contrite.'

'What does the wheel do?' the girl wanted to know.

'Nothing.'

'Nothing! What's the point of that?

'The point is punishment.'

'Until you learn to respect your betters,' Charlie added.

One of the older boys, a fifth former, pointed a finger at Charlie. 'Because you're older than us, doesn't necessarily mean you're better than us.'

'Silence!' Bosch yelled. He peered down at the little girl, eyes blazing with the deadly conviction of a fanatic. 'Up the ladder. Turn the wheel. For all eternity unless you learn genuine contrition. Or even worse, a visit from one of our demonic beasts.'

Terrified of the consequences, the little girl climbed the twenty rungs of the ladder hastily, grabbed the handle of the wheel, and began walking it around in a circle. Bosch aimed a long, thin finger at the fifth form boy. 'And you,' he hissed, 'will move that metal ball up the slope. When it reaches the top, it will roll down again, and then you will repeat the action. On and on and on, forever if necessary, until you learn some manners.'

The fifth former ducked his head, indicating extreme humility, and he looked up at Bosch with an expression of innocence. But it was overdone, and hard to disguise the crafty look in his eyes. 'I've already learnt my lesson. Honestly. I will always stand up for an adult on the bus. And always open doors for others. Help partially sighted people across the road—'

'Enough!' Bosch raised a hand, splaying his fingers. 'I don't believe you. And as for the rest of you—'

The other children cowered, dreading Bosch's terrible punishment. But they didn't discover what damnation their captor was about to dispense, because the little girl turning her wheel was already bored by her task.

'Oh, this is boring!' she moaned, and stopped turning the wheel. 'It's pointless. I'm not doing it anymore.'

Bosch stretched a hand ominously in her direction. 'Little girl,' he roared. 'Judgement day will soon—'

He didn't get a chance to finish because she stamped her foot and said, 'I don't care what happens. I'm not doing it. And you can't make me.'

'Very well,' Bosch laughed evilly, his eyes like molten steel. 'I summon one of purgatory's scaly beasts to devour the transgressor.'

Out of one of the caves came a great lizard-like monster, its head like that of a Pit Bull, slavering jaws dripping saliva hungrily, and a long body of solid armour scales, but with slithery tentacles attached to its monstrous body, with a great pointed tail like that of Satan. The creature from hell moved slowly and menacingly across one of the bridges towards the little girl. She screamed and began to climb down the ladder but had only descended three rungs when the evil creature extended a tentacle, and like a whiplash it encircled the girl's throat. Her scream died with a choking fight for breath, and the monstrous beast jumped onto the wheel, pulling the girl back on to it. It opened its massive mouth, the teeth razor-sharp and dribbling green saliva. In an instant, it clamped its jaws over the girl's head, and snapped them shut. There was a ghastly sound of bones breaking, and the children watched with horror as the terrible beast swallowed the girl's head, and blood poured like a fountain from her severed torso.

Children cried in despair, some of them dropped to their knees, sickened by the sight of their school friend being devoured by the monster. Bosch laughed maniacally, and Charlie shouted, 'Serves her right,' joining Bosch in deranged laughter, which echoed and reverberated insanely around the chamber.

'Mr Griffits! Mr Griffits!'

Charlie felt a hand on his shoulder shaking him out of his deep stupor. He blinked, and the receptionist's face swam into focus.

'I must have nodded off,' he muttered.

The receptionist sighed and shook her head. 'I'm afraid the town hall shuts to visitors at 4.30, and that's in five minutes' time. I'm sorry, but my supervisor was too busy to see you. Besides, I had a word with her about your problem, and she said what I already suspected – nothing we can do about the children occupying the seats. But my supervisor suggested you might write to the bus company.'

'Fat lot of good that'll do,' Charlie grumbled.

'Well, it's worth a try,' she said dismissively, and walked away.

Charlie got up and shuffled slowly and bleary-eyed out of the Town Hall. Muttering as he walked towards the bus stop, telling his dead wife about his dream. 'Who's to say it's not as real as anything else we experience, Rosie? After all, it's in our heads. And that's real enough.'

He stopped talking aloud as he reached the bus stop. An obese woman with a small four-wheel trolley gave him a strange look, and he thought she might have heard him talking to Rosie. But he didn't care.

When the bus came, it was packed with schoolchildren, and he wondered if by sheer chance he might revisit his dream when the bus stooped at Sainsbury's. And if the driver left the bus to relieve himself, then it would be Charlie's golden opportunity to treat these ill-mannered kids to a tearaway drive. He imagined their fearful screams. It was an irresistible thought.

He got on the bus and was confronted by the greatest coincidence of all. The same little boy as the one in his dream stood up and offered him one of the priority seats. Or was his mind playing tricks?

He thanked the boy, and then spotted several middle-aged women with shopping bags standing in the aisles while young children sat in comfort. He felt a swell of anger, turned his head to look towards the back of the bus, and declaimed loudly:

'If the driver needs to relieve himself at Sainsbury's, the next stop for this bus will be purgatory. You're all coming with me to purgatory. Purgatory is next stop after Sainsbury's. Purgatory!'

At the back of the bus, a fifth form boy sniggered, turned to his friend and said, 'We've got the nutter on the bus again.'

10: A Delicacy

The village wasn't far from the high-security psychiatric hospital which housed some of the UK's most evil murderers and rapists. As the hospital, built in the late Victorian era, was six miles from the village, and situated a long way back from the main road, many visitors to the picturesque village gave little thought to the dangerous inmates housed in close proximity to the domestically peaceful teashops of the affectedly middle-England character of the village's main street, as these day trippers ambled through the village, gazing into antique and bric-a-brac shops before succumbing to the temptations of scones and tea cakes in gingham-laden splendour.

It wasn't long after one of the inmates of the hospital committed suicide that Harvey Chimes, a recent resident of the village, discovered what he thought of as an intriguing find – a bargain, in fact – and wondered if it might help him to reflect on the book he was writing about some of Britain's most notorious killers, which was his main reason for moving to the village.

Having moved from the scramble and choking fumes of the big city, his life was now lived at a more leisurely rhythm. And his research and writing about some of the most gruesome and heinous crimes was conducted with a sense of enjoyment, a professionalism and devotion to the task rather than the contemplation of the worst aspects of human behaviour.

His previous publications were non-fiction books, mostly biographies about obscure statesmen and historical figures, which sold reasonably well in a niche market. But he had for years contemplated writing a best-selling work about the infamous. Whenever he discussed it with his wife, she shuddered dramatically and persuaded him to abandon the idea. It was too gruesome to contemplate.

And then two years ago she died in an accident, a fall from a ladder in their back garden. They had one son, who was in this late-thirties and lived and worked in New York, and so Harvey now felt unencumbered and free to write what he damn well felt like writing, sold the city house and moved to the village, to be near to the establishment which housed the worst offenders of human nature. He hoped to be able to interview some of the inmates and form a relationship with a truly evil killer. After all, hadn't Truman Capote struck gold with his non-fiction novel *In Cold Blood* which sold millions and was made into a film.

His terraced cottage was two streets away from the main thoroughfare, at the end of the terrace near a stream and small duckpond. The cottage was small inside, his living room was cluttered, and there were not enough shelves to house all his books, many of which lay scattered on the floor or coffee table, or on the oak table in the small dining area of the L-shaped room. But it was adequate for his needs, and upstairs were two bedrooms, separated by an enormous, airy landing which he used as his working office space, Not that he had done much work so far. Not long after he moved in, he managed to gain access to the high-security hospital and an inmate who agreed to be interviewed. The man was in his late-twenties and was a ruthless murderer who killed everyone in his family, so that he remained the only beneficiary of a substantial estate.

But when Harvey interviewed him, despite all the forensic evidence proving his guilt, he still protested his innocence, and was unforthcoming about his crimes. The author found it a frustrating dead end. If only the evil William Ambrose hadn't committed suicide, Harvey would have loved to interview this serial killer who never pleaded innocence and never once showed remorse.

Up against a recurring writer's block one afternoon, Harvey decided to thoroughly explore his village. Like many charming villages, he knew there was always a downside, and he set out to find it. At one end of the main thoroughfare, there was a garage and petrol station, then beyond it was a road, pitted with potholes, leading to a small council housing estate, with a flat roof pub, at variance with the other two village pubs in the main street that looked as if they accommodated the hunting, shooting, and fishing set. The flat roof pub wasn't overly scruffy, and actually had two colourful hanging baskets outside, but it still didn't look very homely or inviting. Just past the pub, before the semi-circular estate of council houses was a row of shops. A mini-supermarket, a hairdresser, an ironmongers and a junk shop, with all manner of bric-a-brac on the pavement outside.

Intrigued, Harvey entered the shop as a small bell tinkled to announce his entrance. The airless interior smelt musty, of old clothes, wood and dust, and he felt a hay fever-like irritation in his nose. But he was fascinated by the disorderly odds and ends and wondered how anyone could make a living from this junk. There was an old tin bath, and a garden statue of a lion with only half a head, next to a pile of old encyclopaedias and boxes of 78 rpm records nobody could possibly want. But the only thing of interest Harvey could see in the gloom was an enormous stuffed bear by the counter, and behind it a mannequin wearing an old red Household Cavalry uniform.

'Can I help you?'

Harvey started, and his mouth felt suddenly dry. He hadn't noticed the weasel-faced man with the bad comb-over sitting in the shadows behind the counter next to the mannequin.

'Oh – er – I'm just looking.'

'For anything in particular?'

'Well, no, not really.'

Weasel-face sniffed, and his long thin nose looked as if a dew drop might run from the pointed end. But Harvey was relieved to see it remained dry.

'Got some artwork in there,' the proprietor said, pointing to a door frame with no door, just a flimsy curtain masking whatever was in the other room. 'Some interesting paintings.'

Harvey hesitated. Although the shop was full of unsaleable, unusable junk, you just never know when you might stumble on that missing Pissarro or one of Picasso's animal sketches.

But more often than not, just a load of badly-framed reproductions of tat. Still, he was tempted.

The proprietor, seeing Harvey shuffling uncertainly, said, 'What have you got to lose? Might be something of interest. You never know.'

'Yes, of course,' Harvey said decisively. 'I'd like to take a look.'

The proprietor shuffled from behind the counter, old carpet slippers scraping across the concrete floor, and held the curtain back for Harvey to enter. The room was pitch black and the proprietor squeezed past Harvey to switch on a light. A naked bulb hanging on a long flex from the ceiling lit up the gloomy cave of some of the worst art Harvey had ever clapped eyes on. But as his eyes adjusted to the gloom, he spotted a magnificent landscape. It took his breath away it was so stunning. It was a tranquil, snowy scene, and on the left of the picture was an enormous oak tree, its branches covered in snow, and beyond the mighty oak there were more trees in the distance, rising with the hillside, and the perspective was perfect. The snow was pure and undisturbed, not a single animal print to be seen. And yet it was painted with such skill, one could almost see the snow crystals forming each flake. It was an exquisite oil painting and right away he knew he had to have it.

93

The painting was large, in a portrait shape, about six feet in height, and four in width. It would only just fit onto one of the walls of his cottage and, as he stared at the snowy scene, he suddenly felt there was something familiar about it. Almost a feeling of déjà vu.

'Do you recognise the painting?' the proprietor asked.

Harvey shook his head. 'I can't quite—'

'It was in all the newspapers. It was painted by none other than William Ambrose, the serial killer.'

'Yes, of course,' Harvey said, clicking his fingers. 'He spent twenty years on this one painting, and when it was finished he committed suicide. I suppose his life's work was done.'

The proprietor smiled. 'I think the murders were his life's work. Or should I say death's work?'

The weaselly little man continued smiling, but there was little warmth in the smile.

'But how could someone who paints such a beautiful picture murder people in the most gruesome way? The newspapers said that he knocked them out, then crucified them to the floor so there was no escape, and when they came round he pulled out their eyes and ate them, before finishing them off by strangling them with wire. He murdered at least a dozen people and ate their eyes.'

'I think he considered them a delicacy.'

Harvey frowned thoughtfully, then stared at the proprietor with mixed feelings of curiosity and wariness. 'So how did you come by this painting?' he asked.

'William had no family to inherit his final belongings – like this painting. He willed it to me.'

'Did you know each other?'

'We were at school together and remained lifelong buddies.'

'Even though he was a serial murderer?'

'I didn't know that until they caught him.'

'And you never had any suspicions?'

The proprietor stared at Harvey without answering, as if the question was unnecessary. 'No, I suppose not,' Harvey said, feeling the necessity to answer the question on the man's behalf. He looked at the painting again, admiring the perfect layers of paint, and the whiteness of the snow, with delicate touches of colour in places, as if the sun, which could not be seen, had cast its bright rays in small areas that were not shadowed by the trees. Harvey had to admit, the painting was a masterpiece. An evil killer's unique contribution to art, and one the monster had spent twenty years of his incarcerated life painting.

'How much do you want for it?' Harvey asked, thinking as the shop was filled with so much junk, it would go for a song.

'A hundred pounds.'

Harvey whistled and shook his head. 'You're kidding. It's not as if the man is a famous – or even a known – artist.'

'But it is the only painting by a truly evil fiend. It is unique. No one else will be able to claim they have a painting by William Ambrose the serial killer and cannibal.'

'Cannibal?' Harvey questioned, then answered it himself. 'Yes, of course. The eyeballs.'

'So how about it?' the proprietor persisted. 'Are you interested in the purchase or not?'

'Take fifty quid for it?'

The scrawny proprietor ran a hand of blackened fingernails through the few strands of his hair while he thought about this. 'OK,' he answered. 'You drive a hard bargain but fifty quid it is.'

Harvey took out his wallet. 'Oh, no,' he moaned. 'Down to my last twenty. I don't suppose you have a card machine?'

The man stared at him expressionlessly.

Harvey coughed lightly as he cast his eyes around at the junk littering the premises. 'No, I didn't think so. I tell you what: there's an ATM at that little bank in the village. It won't take me long to pop over there and...'

'Oh, that's no good,' the proprietor interrupted. 'During the time you're gone, I might have sold it. Two people, a couple, came in, saw the painting and liked it. They went away to have some tea and to talk it over. So they might come back for it.'

'It will only take me ten minutes to go to the machine and back,' Harvey protested. 'Fifteen at the most.'

The scrawny man shrugged and sniffed. 'Well, you never know. The couple might return during the time you're gone.'

Harvey looked at the painting, and knowing it was painted by one of Britain's most notorious murderer's made it all the more attractive. There was a wheedling tone in his voice when he spoke. 'There must be some way you can help me to buy this painting.'

'I'll tell you what I can do,' the proprietor began, with a sly smile. 'Pay the twenty as a deposit, give me your address, and I will deliver the painting to you. By which time you will have obtained the balance from the bank.'

Harvey hesitated, not certain if he could trust this man. 'Well, if you're sure—'

'I will bring it round to your place when I shut the shop at five-thirty.'

Harvey glanced at the painting again. And that clinched it. He handed the proprietor the twenty pounds, scribbled out his address, tore the page out of the notebook he always carried around with him, and handed it over. 'It's just gone three now, so see you in just over two and a half-hour's time.'

'I will be there. Trust me.'

The way the man hissed the word trust like a slithery snake, gave Harvey a queasy feeling that he was making a foolish purchase. But the deal was done and he was committed, so he hurried to the cash machine to draw out the balance, then went home to await the arrival of the man and the painting.

***

At five-thirty Harvey sat in his landing office, making some final online purchases of some true crime books. It took longer than he anticipated and he had just completed the task fifteen minutes later when there was a knock on his front door. With some excitement, he hurried downstairs and flung open the front door, which opened directly into his living room, and there was the junk shop proprietor, wheezing from the effort of carrying the painting, although it couldn't have been that heavy as it was an unframed canvas.

'Come in,' Harvey gestured, smiling and content now that the seller had kept his word and arrived at the agreed time.

The painting was covered in brown paper, and as soon as the man had put it down, leaning it against a corner of the sofa, Harvey tore off the brown paper. And there it was. The only painting by a serial killer that had been seen in every newspaper in the country and on every television news. And it now belonged to Harvey. A bargain at fifty quid.

He noticed the man's shifty eyes furtively taking in the room, and felt he had to get rid of him as quickly as possible. 'Let me pay you the balance.' He tapped his back pocket for his wallet. Blast! He had left his wallet upstairs when he used his debit card for the online purchases. 'The money's upstairs. I'll get it. Won't take a minute.'

While Harvey was climbing the stairs, the proprietor checked there was a key in the lock of the front door. There was a bunch of keys on the coffee table and one of them looked as if it might be a spare identical door key. He only had seconds so he had to work quickly. He lifted the keys as quietly as possible, struggling to open the metal rings to slide out the key. Then, just as he heard his customer starting back down the stairs, he managed to pocket the spare key and place the bunch back on the table. He doubted the key would be missed. His customer was probably in for the evening now and wouldn't even notice the keys until the next time he went out.

Harvey handed him three ten pound notes, thanked him, and ushered him out. He wouldn't have seen the triumphant and devious grin on the junk man's face who stood outside, because Harvey was transfixed by the painting now, and stood motionless before it, almost as if it was a religious Renaissance painting and he was a devout worshipper. *What a bargain,* he thought. And he fantasised about his true crime best-selling book, being interviewed by the media, and showing-off the painting. And he couldn't wait to hang it in pride of place on the largest wall opposite his sofa from where he could recline and admire it.

First he hurriedly microwaved a ready-meal of lasagne in his small kitchen, ate it hurriedly, and spent the next hour hanging the painting. Then, deciding a celebration was in order, he opened the expensive bottle of malt whisky saved for a special occasion such as this, and sat back on the sofa to toast his success and appreciate the painting.

But the longer he stared at the snowy scene, the more its tranquillity began to bother him. He began to find the view disturbing, and his eye was drawn to the massive oak tree, almost as if something threatening lay behind it. As he downed his third glass of whisky, he chuckled at the stupid unease he felt. It was only a painting. But the more he drank, and the more he stared at the painting, the more agitated he became. His eyes became heavier and he managed to pour himself one more glass, the last in the bottle.

His eyes closed. And then he experienced an enormous bang deep inside his head, with a pain like the worst hangover he had ever experienced, as a painful hammer blow in his head pounded out excruciating damage to his brain. Then more hammering, and a screeching sound like rough metal scraping on steel, and although he wasn't fully conscious, he felt his body shivering feverishly as hot and icy blades of pain shot up and down his spine.

He could have sworn he felt a hand gently tapping his cheek, bringing him round. He groaned and opened his eyes, tried to speak but was gagged with a plastic strip. And then the evil killer's face appeared close to his. It was the face of evil. William Ambrose, who should have been dead. And here was the monster bending over him, peering at him like a specimen. The fiend's face was round, fat and pasty, with double chins hanging loosely, and wide nostrils, bushy eyebrows and grey eyes as cold as glass marbles, containing not a spark of humanity.

With a great effort Harvey turned his head away from the heavily-breathing savage and, as he did so, it was with horror that he saw the spike impaling one of his hands to the floor. Which was when the excruciating pain in the palms of his hands throbbed and burned like hot coals. He squirmed and struggled, attempting to wriggle free of his restraints, but the more he struggled the more agonizing the pain became in his hands. And then his head was turned roughly around so that he faced the fiend, who grinned and moved even closer. Harvey cringed away from the evil monster's thumb and forefinger as it moved towards his right eye. He screamed through the plastic gag as he felt the long fingernails pressing into his eye socket. The pain was unbelievable as the fiend removed his eyeball. He screamed though his gag and his left eye flicked open involuntarily. That was when he saw his exterminator chewing on his eyeball. He screamed again, but the sound was muffled by the gag, and again he felt the rummaging fingers delving into his left eye socket. His throat raw from screaming, he then felt the wire sliding around his neck, and he knew beyond doubt that his death was inevitable.

***

Early the following morning, the junk man let himself into Harvey's cottage. He hadn't needed the key after all, because the door was unlocked. He gave a self-satisfied smirk as he stopped to look at his customer's corpse in its crucified position on the floor, pools of blood from the pinioned hands staining the rug. The corpse's eyelids were shut but he didn't need to raise them to know that his friend had enjoyed his delicate little snack.

Stepping over the corpse, he moved towards the wall on which the painting hung and raised it from its picture hook. He carried it towards the door, stopping just before he left to take another brief look at the corpse. It had worked. Even beyond death, his friend was active once more.

He shut and locked the door behind him, and as he walked back through the village towards his junkshop, he wondered how long it would be before the corpse was discovered. He chuckled as he imagined the polices' reaction on discovering the crime used the same modus operandi as his friend's insatiable murders. They would no doubt come to the conclusion that this was a copycat murder. And how wrong they would be.

Back at his shop, he was about to take the painting into the other room but changed his mind. Instead, he placed it on the counter next to the uniformed mannequin so that customers hoping for a bargain would instantly be attracted to his friend's painting as soon as they entered.

He stood back to admire his friend's work and smiled as he saw that now there was something very different about the painting. From behind the oak tree there came footprints. Now there were footprints in the snow.

11: The Wager

It was a quiet morning, sunny but not too hot on that late spring day in Crowfield as I typed out a report on last night's arrest. Another drunk and disorderly, leading to an affray, and the culprit was none other than that usual suspect Arnie Wilmings. If I had a dollar for the all the times I arrested him for disturbing the peace, I reckon I'd be driving my own Cadillac by now.

The thing about Arnie is, he's not a bad man, just can't take his liquor. The booze turns him into a monster, a sort of Jekyll and Hyde scenario, and whenever I arrest him I get racially insulted. He's one of the few citizens of this small town in Barron County, Mississippi, who has yet to reconcile himself to the changing times and being arrested by a black police officer.

But Arnie's one of only a few in Barron County to hold any sort of prejudice, and that's when he's drunk, and he is generally mortified the next morning, always claiming he can't remember anything. Most people in the county, with a population of only 42,000, are friendly and hospitable, and in Crowfield the community is close-knit.

Once I finished my report, I poured myself a coffee just as Dion arrived back at the station.

'Looks like I got back the right time,' he said with a grin.

I handed him a cup, saying, 'Help yourself to cream,' and went back and sat at my desk.

Dion sat at the desk opposite mine and toasted me with the coffee. Dion's younger than me, is what you might call a rookie, and has only been in the job less than three months. He's fresh-faced, still looks like a high school kid, and bears a passing resemblance to Meatloaf.

'You heard about the latest haunting at the Hereford Plantation?' Dion said with a certain relish.

I wondered whether he said it to wind me up, knowing how much I hate superstitious nonsense like belief in ghosts. I shook my head, refusing to be drawn into this web of nonsense.

'Man who heard 'bout the haunting come all the way from Atlanta to take the challenge.'

'More fool him,' I said.

'Seems he was scared out of his wits. Normal young guy one minute then—' Dion paused, flicked out his fingers like a magician performing a trick. 'Now he's a headcase. Don't know what day it is. Seeing a shrink.'

I laughed. 'He must have had a screw loose to begin with then.'

Dion looked at me suspiciously, screwing up his eyes. 'Don't tell me all them people been freaked out at the Plantation are just… just…'

'Just plain gullible,' I said. 'When they go in and see that monster's portrait hanging on the wall, their minds get signals.'

'You mean from beyond the grave?'

'No, from their subconscious minds. And the right cerebral hemisphere of the brain dominates the reasoning left one and is swamped by their emotions.'

Dion's jaw dropped. 'How do you know that?'

'Scientific fact.'

'I never paid no attention to science at school. My folks is religious. They put their trust in Christianity not all that Big Bang hooey.'

Not wanting to admit just how religious my folks are too, I kept quiet. Growing up, I always attended church with them, but I think they guessed the church was gradually losing me as I became more interested in scientific subjects at high school. Mealtimes sometimes became something of a strain and led to arguments.

'So, you reckon all them ghosts 'n' hauntings can be explained scientifically?' Dion prodded.

'Not always explained. There are some mysteries remain mysteries. Which doesn't mean they are supernatural. Could be other explanations.'

'You don't think Bradley Quayle was such an evil man his tormented spirit haunts that house?'

Bradley Quayle, notorious owner of the Hereford Plantation, was one of the 19th century's cruellest of men. He frequently flogged his slaves unmercifully, used torture to destroy any who were unfit to work, and routinely used the women to indulge in the most perverted sexual practises. In 1849, a slave whose wife had been subjected to the most degrading and humiliating of Quayle's twisted vices, lost his mind and killed the Plantation owner. In retribution for the homicide, he and six other slaves were hanged from trees in the Plantation grounds.

I shivered as I recalled Quayle's barbaric history, and said to Dion, 'I think anyone knowing of Quayle's evil, and spending a night there, might be scared and unable to sleep. They might suffer the most terrible nightmares, which would be understandable. I don't think these are supernatural apparitions.'

I noticed a sly smile on Dion's face and wondered what was coming next.

'So, you think you could spend the night there and not worry?'

'Even knowing the terrible history of the place, it wouldn't put a scare on me.'

'Hundred dollars says you can't do it without getting the heebie-jeebies.'

Dion grinned hugely, and I knew he'd got me. He knows my weakness. I can't see two flies walking up a windowpane without betting on which one reaches the top. I'll bet on anything. Some are addicted to alcohol, others its drugs or sex. My addiction is gambling, and Dion knew that, and capitalized on it. Whether it was to prove a point or thinking he might make some easy money if I ended up being terrified during a night spent at the Plantation, I wasn't certain.

But I took the bet.

***

If you've ever seen *Gone With The Wind*, you'll have some idea of what the Hereford Plantation Museum looks like, with its long drive up to the mansion, with tall white pillars like some Greek temple. As I drove up, Jamie Lee Blake, the curator, was expecting me, and he and Dion's Aunt Mary, who worked as Jamie Lee's secretary, were waiting outside to greet me. Dion couldn't make it as it was a Saturday night, and he needed to police the town. I was also on call, but I didn't think the usual suspected drunks were anything Dion couldn't handle on his own, so I was expecting to get an undisturbed night's sleep and pick up an easy hundred dollars. Which would teach Dion a lesson, not only about gambling, but also about superstition.

I grabbed my overnight bag from the back seat of the car and walked up the steps to meet them.

'Hi there, Marvin,' Jamie Lee said, and we shook hands. 'You sure about this?'

I laughed and said, 'Just trying to prove a point about superstition.'

I kissed Mary's cheek. She seemed subdued and I asked her what was wrong.

'I don't like this. Never have done. In fact, if I had my way, I'd burn that evil man's portrait. I keep telling Jamie Lee to burn it. Get rid of it. But he won't listen.'

Jamie Lee chuckled. 'Marvin's a tough officer, Mary. I'm sure he'll be fine.'

'You've worked here for many years, Mary,' I said, 'and I don't think I ever heard of you being frightened.'

I saw her shiver.

'No, but I ain't ever been on my own up in that master bedroom, with his portrait hanging in the hall outside. I sticks to Jamie Lee's office, 'less I occasionally takes a party of people up there.'

'Safety in numbers?' I said.

'Something like that. Well, if you don't mind, Jamie Lee, I'll get off home.' She threw me a worried glance, muttering, 'Bye, Marvin. Good luck.'

'Shall we go inside,' Jamie Lee gestured, and I walked in front of him and into the vast hall, with its impressive chandelier, sweeping staircase and marble pillars. He showed me into his office, a large room with an ornate cornice painted a slightly darker blue then the powder blue of the walls. It looked as if it was once a grander room in the house, but was now an ordinary office, containing a large desk and all the usual office paraphernalia. Although I had visited the house before, I had never been in the office and I noticed along one wall was a single divan bed.

Jamie Lee caught me looking at it and explained, 'If someone is staying on the premises, as you are, for insurance purposes I or an employee of the Hereford has to be here too.'

I slapped my forehead. 'I'm sorry. I've really inconvenienced you with this ridiculous stunt. When you could be at home with your family on a Saturday night.'

'They're used to it. I get many visits from ghost hunters, all wanting to take the challenge of sleeping in that room.'

'And are they all freaked out by it?'

Jamie Lee laughed. 'Far from it. Some go away disappointed. You only hear about the ones who claim they saw Bradley Quayle terrifying them. I don't believe it myself, but I hate that portrait of him. I should have destroyed that years ago.'

'Isn't that like air-brushing history?'

'Maybe. But here we focus on the history of slavery. We focus on where they came from, how they got here, and how they suffered on the Plantation. And I have another reason for wanting to get rid of the portrait. We sometimes get visitors who are fascinated by the cruelty of the man. I guess they are attracted by the violence and the glamour of the way the Plantation owners lived.'

'A bit like people who are fascinated by Nazi uniforms and that sort of memorabilia?'

'Exactly.'

It was just gone eight p.m. when Jamie Lee and I settled down in his office and chatted for the next two hours. He brought out two glasses and a bottle of bourbon from the cupboard to help pass the time convivially. I'm not much of a drinker and stuck to just the one glass. Just after ten o'clock I said I thought I was ready to turn-in.

'You sure about this?' Jamie Lee asked me.

I gave him a confident smile. 'I'm a complete sceptic. And sceptics do not see ghosts. They do not exist as far as sceptics are concerned.'

'So why are you doing this? You never told me.'

'It was Mary's nephew Dion challenged me. He believes in all that guff.'

'And you want to prove him wrong?'

'I will prove him wrong.'

'Well, let's hope you're right. OK. We'll go up, shall we?'

I picked up my overnight bag and he led the way upstairs, then along hallways with high windows, heavy with brocade curtains, and walls festooned with tapestries and portraits of Bradley Quayle's family. When we reached the East Wing and saw the master bedroom door at the end of a long corridor, Jamie Lee stopped, and I followed his gaze as he looked up at the portrait hanging on the wall. It was enormous. Bradley Quayle stared down at us, his eyes evil and penetrating. I wondered who the artist was and if he'd been freaked out by the commission.

There was no denying the evil inherent in the man whose image had been captured by the artist. The thin lips sneered arrogantly, and you could read in the eyes the man's thoughts, how distorted and twisted they were. It was only a portrait, yet I felt he wanted to abuse me for his own sadistic pleasure. He wore a long jacket, and a fancy waistcoat with a bootlace tie. On his hip a gun belt and a Colt .45. His hand hovered over the revolver like a gunslinger from the old Wild West. But those details were nothing compared to the cold evil in his eyes. I felt I was looking into the face of the devil.

'See what I mean about evil fascination with his portrait,' Jamie Lee said, breaking the deathly silence of our observation.

'I can see how charming he ain't,' I said. 'Enough to give you the creeps. But I'll try not to let it freak me out.'

Jamie Lee pushed open the door to the master bedroom and ushered me in. Never have I seen such an extravagant bedroom in real life before. This was like pictures I'd seen of royal bedrooms in England and France. The furniture alone must have been worth a small fortune, and the four-poster bed's canopy was made of fine silk in a multitude of colours.

I heard Jamie Lee chuckle. 'Think you'll be comfortable in here?'

I turned to see the amused look on his face and I just wondered for a moment whether this was because a black police officer would soon be sleeping in a bigoted, slave-owning tyrant's bed.

'As long as the spirits of the dead don't rise up. I think I'm in for a good night's sleep.'

Jamie Lee gestured at a door which was roped off. 'There is the master's en suite bathroom you can use – just unclip the rope. When visitors go around, we keep it roped off with the door open, so they can look inside, but are discouraged from using it. But feel free to use it yourself.'

'Thanks. I appreciate the hospitality, Jamie Lee.'

He wished me a good night's sleep, and then left me to it.

After brushing my teeth in a bathroom that must have had more space in it than my bungalow, I got undressed, into my pyjamas, and slid between the sheets of the four-poster. Out of habit, I unholstered my Glock and placed it on the large oak cabinet next to the bed. It was something I have always done, ever since I was attacked one night by an intruder, intent on murdering me for arresting his brother for armed robbery. I managed to disarm the man, and I'm proud to say I have only ever fired my sidearm in the shooting gallery.

Although I was tired, I read for a while, a non-fiction book about artificial intelligence. Soon my eyelids became heavy and I stopped absorbing what I read. I put down the book and turned off the light. I lay for a moment, my eyes adjusting to the dark, and listened for any random noises. But everything was quiet. *Deathly quiet* a voice taunted me in my head. I chased the voice away, and then I don't remember falling asleep.

I woke up with a start, like something had startled me in my sleep. Maybe it was a strange dream I had difficulty remembering. For a moment I was disorientated, then remembered where I was. I listened for any disturbing noises and told myself that I was being stupid. Ghosts? No way. Just manifestations of the mind.

Still wearing my wristwatch, I checked the luminous dial. Just after two a.m.

And then came the creaking of footsteps along the hall. Just outside the door. It had to be an intruder, I told myself.

I was suddenly wide awake. Could I hear someone breathing or was this my own shallow breath? I sat up, staring at the door, peering through the darkness. Certain I could hear something, my unease grew as I waited, almost expecting the door handle to turn. Breathing evenly, this is no ghost I told myself. It must be an intruder. I felt for my gun and picked it up.

I waited. Waited for the door to open. And then I heard it. A terrible laugh. A cruel, mocking laugh. And that was when the figure burst through the door. I could swear it was Quayle, and I saw the hatred in his eyes, evil like deadly venom burning in those terrible eyes as he moved towards me, his hand reaching for the revolver in his holster. But what was so horrific was the demonic force of his presence. This man was from hell itself, spewing hatred, creeping towards me like an ugly fiend.

'Stop!' I shouted. 'Don't come any closer or I'll shoot.'

But the sadistic monster, crept even closer.

I pulled the trigger. The shot rang out and I must have hit him in the chest. Still he came towards me. I pulled the trigger again, this time a shot to the head.

I froze. Stared at Quayle, watching as he cried in agony, as if he was being murdered all over again. Perhaps it was his punishment which would go on for eternity, reliving the slave's revenge for all his barbarous acts.

And then, as the apparition vanished, along with his declining, deathly groan, my extreme foolishness hit me like a ramrod. I was just as gullible as all the rest. Because of that portrait, and knowing the history of the evil tyrant, my mind created him. That was the only explanation. And now, stupidly, I had fired two rounds at my imagination.

Jesus! How embarrassing.

And how the hell could I explain my behaviour to Dion? And Jamie Lee, and Dion's Aunt Mary, not to mention anyone else in Crowfield who listened to gossip?

It wasn't long before I heard Jamie Lee hurrying along the hall outside. 'Marvin! What's happening. I heard shots. You OK?'

I got up and opened the door. Jamie Lee had switched on all the lights in the hall.

'What happened, Marvin?'

I was embarrassed. I didn't want to admit I'd seen Quayle.

'I thought I heard an intruder.'

'And you took a couple of shots at this – er – intruder?'

'Yes. I may have been mistaken. I'm sorry. And I'm sorry that I woke you.'

Jamie Lee tilted his head, gave me a strange look. 'You saw Quayle, didn't you?'

'Well, I—' I began, and felt the heat in my cheeks. 'If I did, it was purely my imagination. I thought it was an intruder you see, coming into the bedroom. I warned whoever it was not to come any closer. I couldn't see clearly in the dark, and they kept coming towards me, and that's when I let off two rounds.'

'I think,' Jamie Lee said, 'you must have been sleepwalking.'

I shook my head as I tried to remember. 'No, I don't think so. I never left the bedroom. That was when I thought I shot the intruder.'

He grabbed my arm and took me a couple of paces towards the portrait. 'Then how do you explain this?'

I looked up at Quayle's portrait, and there in the middle of his chest was a large bullet hole. And another one in his head.

'But that's not possible,' I cried. 'I definitely took the shots in the bedroom.'

Jamie Lee sighed and shook his head. 'That's not possible, Marvin. You must have been sleepwalking.'

'Wait a minute.' I looked down at the floor. 'Where are the spent casings? The ejected casings should be here if I fired my gun in the hall.'

We tore into the bedroom and checked the area around the bed. Sure enough, the ejected casings were on the floor. I felt my throat constrict.

'But I don't understand,' I rasped.

Jamie Lee placed an arm around my shoulder. 'It's that demon – Quayle.'

'It can't be,' I protested. 'I can't believe that.'

He moved me towards the bed and sat me on the edge.

'I know you've had a shock, Marvin. Just take it easy. Relax. Try not to think about what's happened. I'm going to do something I should have done years ago. I'm going to burn that cursed portrait.'

He hurried from the room, while I sat with my head in my hands. I suppose I was in a state of shock. I vaguely heard a noise from the hall, and presumed it was Jamie Lee dealing with the painting. I don't know how long I sat there recovering. It could have been just a few minutes, or a great deal longer. Eventually, I got a grip on myself and walked out into the hall. I looked at the faded wallpaper and the outline of where the painting had hung. Staring at it stupidly, I suddenly realised what was wrong. There should have been two bullet holes in the wall. If the shots had hit the painting, there should have been two slugs in the wall.

This was crazy.

I went back into the bedroom and checked the door. There were two bullet holes and slugs in the door where I had fired the gun. *Jesus!* It was macabre. I had fired my gun at what I thought was Quayle's apparition, but there were also two holes in the painting. But no holes on the wall behind it.

How was this possible?

And then I realised Jamie Lee had gone downstairs to burn the painting. I had to stop him. I couldn't let him destroy the only proof we had that this bizarre occurrence was something both of us had witnessed.

I found him in the grounds near the vegetable garden, shining a torch on a bonfire he had lit. Watching as the flames consumed the last of the evil slave master.

'I wanted to stop you,' I said breathlessly. 'It was the only proof we had that we weren't going mad.'

He shrugged. 'It's better this way. And, to explain the bullet holes on the door, let's stick to the story that you had a nightmare – thought you saw that evil monster – and tried to plug him.'

'People won't respect a police officer who shoots ghosts,' I said.

'I wouldn't worry about that,' he said. 'People want to believe in ghosts. They won't lose any respect for a man who has a supernatural experience. If anything, they'll be jealous. But I guess you owe Dion the bet.'

I was surprised he knew about the wager and wondered if Dion had blabbed.

'How did you know about the wager? Did Dion tell you?'

He shook his head. 'It's a small town. We're all aware of your addiction, officer.'

***

When Dion got into the station early Monday morning, he had a huge grin on his face. I was already prepared for this, and I had the hundred in ten-dollar bills sitting on my desk.

'I guess your Saturday night was as eventful as mine,' he chortled. 'Shooting at ghosts, eh? Which must mean you believed the thing was real.'

'I admit,' I said, 'there was a weird sensation – something not quite right about the place. It must've played on my mind.'

'D'you often shoot things you see in your mind?

'OK. You win your hundred bucks. Now can we drop the subject?' I could see by the triumphant grin on his face that he was about to continue with some banter, so I hurriedly changed the subject. 'You said you also had an eventful Saturday night. What happened?'

'Just the usual. Arnie Wilmings drunk again. And I got me a stream of racial abuse.'

'Wait a minute. Arnie is white, and you are white. So, what's with the racial abuse?'

'He was so drunk he didn't know who arrested him.'

Despite surrogate insults from the town's bigot, I had to laugh. I opened my desk drawer and took out a deck of playing cards. Dion stared at me with a mixture of confusion and suspicion.

'What's with the cards, man?'

I pushed the hundred bucks across the desk, next to the cards. 'Cut the cards. Ace high. Highest card wins.'

'What are we playing for?'

I nodded at the money. 'Double or quits?'

I could see the temptation unfolding in his eyes. The irresistible greed of all us gamblers. And I knew then that I had him.

12: Metal Fiend

I retired as Forensic Team Manager last week, and it's only now after almost forty years that I feel ready to write about the way I helped the police to catch a serial killer. This was from my one anonymous phone call back in 1979, after simple experiments became nightmares as an evil monster trespassed in my head during an ESP experiment – an experience I never spoke about, other than to my wife Sue, years later.

I was a university student at the time, studying criminology. Two years after my graduation I joined a team of forensic scientists and, because of the nature of the work, I never told anyone about my bizarre experience. I was reluctant to admit having what amounted to an occult visitation in my brain. I always felt, as I'm sure most of my colleagues did, that forensic scientists should be pragmatic and clear-sighted, and admitting to having submitted to the unfamiliar territory of extrasensory perception and experiencing a macabre manifestation would be unwise. Many scientists regarded extrasensory perception as preposterous, a steppingstone in the direction of the supernatural, a dabbling with the occult. But in the sixties things began to change, especially when theoretical physics became ever more complex.

Because of my studies, and my interest in physics, especially Heisenberg's Uncertainty Principle, basically positing the theory that there is no way to precisely measure essential properties of subatomic behaviour, I began to consider the possibility of parapsychology and telepathy as biological radio transmissions, as did many other reputable scientists.

When an eminent professor of the science faculty appealed for guinea pigs for long and sometimes tedious experiments in telepathy, I volunteered as a subject, as did several other students. Although I was still rather sceptical, feeling it was a step too close to spiritualism, I was nevertheless curious, and young and naïve enough to think it might help me in criminology, especially if I decided to go down the route of criminal profiling. Little did I know as I allowed myself to drift into this strange area of the mind, how I would have to bury this experience and pretend it never happened.

Professor Stella Raquin, conducting the experiments, was an attractive woman in her mid-thirties. At first, we were involved in basic psychokinetic experiments, attempting to use our minds to influence inanimate objects. I found if I rolled dice, relaxed and didn't think too hard, I could often predict the numbers, and the mathematical results were good, my scores displaying far better outcomes than pure chance. We spent many weeks of our spare time conducting experiments in random card guessing, and Professor Raquin was almost fanatical in her devotion to mathematical analysis. After what seemed like months spent guessing which card would be turned up with thousands upon thousands of attempts at telepathic predictions, she decided it was time to move on to communication between a sender of images and a recipient. I had scored highly at dice and card guessing, as had Adrian, another science student, and we were chosen for the next experiment. We were given separate rooms in which to sit, rooms which were devoid of character, bare except for modest tables and chairs. There was also a green light at my table which lit up as Adrian attempted to send me an image telepathically, which would then be switched off until he was ready to transmit the next image.

Professor Raquin, it was decided, would spend half the time observing me, and the other half observing Adrian, alternating with Dr Roger Harden, a psychologist. We were given felt tip pens and paper, and Adrian was instructed to freely improvise the drawing of images on to a sheet of paper, which he would then try to communicate telepathically to me.

I had been told to relax, and empty my mind of any distractions, such as trivial worries or concerns about my criminology course. The first image I drew resembled a wine glass, then the light went off and I waited for it to come on again. As soon as it lit up an image came into my head instantly. A straight horizontal line, with a smaller vertical line beneath it, like an oversize letter T. I drew the image quickly and the light went off again. As soon as it came back on I saw nothing. Instead, darkness. Then a terrible noise in my head filled the vacuum. A disturbing sound, reverberating and screaming. Gradually images appeared through the cloud of noise, blood red, and an enlarged mouth, screaming wildly. I put my hands over my ears, tried to stop the blood-curdling scream and the pulsating bass noise of a heartbeat, beating against my own heart rate.

I must have been shaking and showing signs of distress, because Professor Raquin put down her notes, came over to me and asked if I was all right. I told her I was fine and had just experienced a bad dream. I was so relaxed, I said, that I almost drifted off to sleep, which was when I suffered the nightmare.

'Michael,' she said. 'What happened to you? Tell me.'

I could tell by her voice, although she tried to disguise it, that she was intrigued, and wanted to know more, hoping I might have experienced a biological radio transmission, which was what these experiments were all about. But I found the images in my head so disturbing, I lied and said it was just tiredness from overwork.

He catches up with her at the edge of the park. As she turns and sees him, her mouth opens in fear. Maybe she screams, but he can't hear her because the music is pounding in his head. Frantic, intense and feverish. Feeding his anger. He feels an almighty pain in his fist as he slams it into her mouth. He drags her into the bushes. Now he can do whatever he wants with her. Then afterwards, the knife sharpened and ready in his anorak pocket, he'll finish her off.

That first session of our psychical research continued after I recovered, and I thought no more about that brief but vivid nightmare. The results, after Professor Raquin and Dr Harden checked our images, were startlingly precise. Seven out of every twelve of my drawings pretty much resembled Adrian's, and in the order in which he sent them. And two of the images, one of a fish, and the other of a circle with a cross on top like an orb, were so accurate that we were all stunned, never expecting such accuracy. And we had spent three hours and drawn at least two hundred images.

To hit one playing card out of five possibles was one thing, but to accurately produce images from an infinite number of designs was quite another. But Professor Raquin and Dr Harden seemed less excited by the results and wanted another session. Adrian and I were surprised by their cautious and non-committal attitude to what seemed to me almost proof positive that ESP figured in the great scheme of things.

We arranged another session for a week later.

As I continued with my criminology studies the following day, I became fascinated by a rape and murder that hit the headlines. It happened in a small park in Portsmouth, and the victim was a girl of nineteen, a shop assistant on her way home after late-night closing. It was a Thursday, the same night we had the experimental ESP session. At the time I made no connection between the two events, and I was more interested in the rape and murder from a forensic angle and followed the story as it unfolded.

But over the course of the week, as I read the latest reports of the gruesome murder, the police arrested no suspects and their investigation seemed to hit a brick wall.

The following Thursday we sat in our spartan rooms and began our session just before nine p.m. This time the session began with Dr Harden in my room and Professor Raquin in Adrian's, and it was arranged that they would switch places halfway through the session as they had the week previously and compare the images then.

Feeling relaxed and freeing my mind from the stresses of everyday problems, the session became a form of meditation as I scrawled images with a black felt tip. I had been at it for about half an hour when I felt a sudden jarring sensation. A spasm racked my body and a loud screech in my brain was like a knife slicing into my throat. I thought I saw a bloodied mouth, screaming with fear as a cymbal crashed. And then I heard more clearly a human voice: *I laugh when I'm creeping.*

A hand on my shoulder, shaking me back to normality. It was Dr Harden, asking me if I was all right.

I assured him it was nothing, although I was shaken by the images I'd received. I asked if we could break for ten minutes, which gave me an opportunity to see what was in Adrian's head at the time.

Nothing was the answer. Other than the random images he sent.

We continued with the session, and the results were pretty much the same as before, giving us good scores, indicating that the results showed positive connections between us rather than coincidence.

Professor Raquin now thought the results were so good that she and Dr Harden agreed that we would have one more session a week later, and they would write up the results in a paper.

I was now less sceptical and thought the results so far demonstrated there was good reason to believe in telepathy.

And then, when I began to think seriously about the interruptions in the session, the frightening images and voices in my head, I realised I had an even greater reason to believe.

Friday morning the news on the radio brought the shocking report of another murder, this one in Southsea, which I discovered is a district of Portsmouth. This was also a young woman in her late twenties, who was attacked brutally on her way home from the cinema, having just said goodbye to her friend. She was dragged into an alley, brutally beaten senseless, raped and then had her throat cut. The murderer also slashed her in the groin area after killing her. Now the police warned the public that this looked like the work of a serial killer, and the knifing of the girl in the groin area looked as if the perpetrator was taking Jack the Ripper as inspiration for his evil acts.

I still didn't make the connection between the images and voices in my head and the murders. At least, my consciousness ignored it, while I think my subconscious worked hard to make the link. I could still hear clearly in my memory that mocking voice: *I laugh when I'm creeping.* And I guessed, because of all the noisy accompaniment, that it may have been a song lyric, even though its clarity had been strangled by the high-pitched screams.

I started to ask around the campus, and the students' union bar, if anyone could identify the lyric for me. There were some students who had formed their own band, and it was their drummer who gave me the answer.

The song was 'The Ripper' by Judas Priest, a song about Jack the Ripper.

I almost dreaded the next ESP session. Fearing the voices and screams in my head, as soon as the session began I broke out in a sweat, shivering and hot, as if I was coming down with a bout of flu. None of Adrian's images made much sense, and my pen scribbled nothing but black messy daubs. And then came the high-pitched screaming in my head, blood-spurting images and cries of fear and pain, as I heard once more a mocking voice chanting *Highway to Hell… Highway to Hell.*

I was so distressed I asked if we could end the ESP session, telling Professor Raquin that I felt ill. She looked at me suspiciously, asked if it was anything to do with the messages I received. I didn't want to appear foolish, so I lied, telling her it had nothing to do with the sessions and was probably something I ate.

The next morning, I dreaded turning the radio on. When I did, even though I half expected the devastating news, it still came as a shock.

The third murder, this time a fifteen-year-old schoolgirl, was murdered in the same way but in Southampton, which was only a little distance from Portsmouth. The killing showed all the symptoms of a deranged Ripper copycat killing, although the stabbing in the groin area was done messily and hurriedly.

Receiving these messages connected to the murders had me thinking I was going crazy. And then it occurred to me that I ought to do something about it. First, I asked about the last voice I'd heard. Most students informed me that 'Highway to Hell' was sung by an Australian heavy metal band called AC/DC.

Heavy metal. It looked as if the murderer was a heavy metal freak. But why did snatches of those songs coincide with images of the victims in distress?

And then, as I sat in the union bar that evening, I spotted a student listening to music on his Sony Walkman. Of course! The latest gadget. These portable audio-cassette players were all the rage. Perhaps the murderer owned one and played heavy metal tracks while he raped and knifed his victims.

But even if I had guessed the truth, what the hell could I do with this information? I couldn't go to the police and tell them I'd had a psychic message telling me the murderer was a heavy metal freak. They'd think I was mad, and I couldn't blame them. I wondered if I ought to confide in Professor Raquin. She'd seen the way I'd been affected by something during the ESP sessions. And what if she believed me? What then?

Confiding in Professor Raquin, I decided, was a bad move. I was studying criminology not mumbo-jumbo. If I got a reputation as a superstitious lunatic, it could have serious repercussions on my future career.

But it was now three weeks since the first murder, and still the police hadn't apprehended a suspect. Maybe I was the only person in the country with information that could lead them to an arrest. Now I began to hear a different voice in my head. The voice of my conscience telling me that I needed to act on the information I had been given, however bizarre that might seem.

I took the easy way out. I decided it would have to be an anonymous phone call to the police. Cowardly, I know. But what if the newspapers got hold of the story of my freakish messages? I would be branded an idiot, using mumbo-jumbo to solve a heinous crime. Not good for a career as a scene of crime officer, even if it helped to solve the crime. They would think of the heavy metal connection as nothing more than coincidence. A crank's strange dream. I would become a laughingstock.

I got the number of Portsmouth Central Police Station from Directory Enquiries and phoned from a callbox. When the operator answered, I asked to be put through to the team investigating the recent rapes and murders. She asked for my name and number, so I gave her a false name and the call box number, because I didn't plan to hang around once I had given a detective my information. She connected me to the incident room. I guessed they get many crank phone calls, but they must take every call seriously, in case an eyewitness recalls someone acting suspiciously. Even though this happened almost forty years ago, I can recall the conversation in detail.

'Mr Jackson?' said the youthful voice. 'Detective Constable Wilmot here. I believe you have information regarding the recent murders.'

'It's possible,' I said, 'that these crimes have been committed by a heavy metal freak. And the perpetrator listens to these songs on his Walkman while he rapes and kills his victims.'

'Listens on what? I didn't catch that.'

'A Walkman. You know, a portable audio cassette player.'

'Could I ask you, sir, how you came by this information?'

'I'm a criminal profiler,' I lied. 'Please don't dismiss this as a crank call. I urge you to look into someone who has purchased heavy metal tapes, and it's possible he may own a Walkman.'

'Yes, but where—' he started to say, but the line went dead as I slammed the phone down and left the callbox.

Having made the anonymous call, I felt I had in some way acquitted myself of any lack of moral duty. If the images that bombarded my brain during the ESP sessions had been nothing but nonsense, then there was no real harm done. The police, according to the newspapers, hadn't unearthed any clues as to the identity of any suspects, so my call was hardly wasting police time, even if my sixth sense turned out to be nothing more than hocus-pocus.

Nothing happened for three or four days. Then, just before the weekend, it was big news that a man had been charged for the murders. Apparently, detectives had traced him through credit card purchases he made at record stores. He was a heavy metal freak, and his flat was decorated with posters of extreme violence, Nazi propaganda and Satanism. He also owned a Walkman.

Of course, there was no mention of the anonymous tip-off. And maybe the young detective could claim all the credit for the result. But at least I felt absolved of any guilt I might have suffered had my information been ignored.

I followed the case avidly, right up to and throughout the trial, when the murderer, a man named Neil Cannery, an unemployed loner in his early thirties, was sentenced to a term of life in a hospital for the criminally insane, so it was possible he might never be released.

After it was all over, I erased the memory of those ESP sessions and refused to confront any lingering echoes of those horrendous images. And I never thought any more about it until our son, Mark, when he was 14-years-old, began collecting heavy metal CDs, which he often played in the evenings. I used to go berserk and would storm out of the house whenever he played Motörhead, Black Sabbath and various other metal bands. Mark, my daughter Julie and Sue wondered why I behaved so irrationally and childishly, refusing to return from the pub until there was another genre of music being played.

It was then I confided in Sue, told her the story of the murders, and how my psychic experiences with the heavy metal sounds may have helped to solve the dreadful crimes.

Sue urged me to tell our children, but I resisted. By the time they were in their teens, I had risen to manager of our forensic team, and I suppose I wanted them to look up to me as a scientist, rather than as a man who once dabbled in the occult. Besides, as they grew older, their music tastes changed, and they eventually left for university and made lives of their own.

Now that I've retired, I may tell them. And it's only since my retirement that I feel able to write this account.

Only a few weeks after my retirement party, I thought about Neil Cannery. It was almost forty years ago, and I couldn't help wondering if there had been any change in his circumstances, was he capable of being rehabilitated and might he be eligible for parole?

And then one night he invaded my brain once more. I remembered a gong banging in my head, getting louder and louder, and a terrible voice threatening death. My hand clutched my throat and a I felt as if I was choking. I woke up screaming, and Sue held me close, knowing I'd had a terrible nightmare.

'You've just had a bad dream, my darling,' she whispered.

Shaking my head, I said, 'It was no dream. It was like going back forty years and reliving that terrible psychic experience. And there was the start of a song I recognised. It was one Mark often played. One that drove me out to the pub.'

Sue laughed as she smoothed my forehead and kissed me gently. 'As if you needed an excuse to go to the pub.'

'No, the song is 'Death', I'm sure of it, from an album called Nostradamus by Judas Priest. Why did it invade my sleep now, of all times? All the terrible crime scenes I've visited over the years have never affected me. So why this visitation now, like I was back in that murderer's head?'

I heard Sue's restrained sigh. 'It's just a bad dream, darling. Forget it, and let's go back to sleep.'

But I couldn't forget it. It was another disturbing visitation, and I dreaded listening to the early morning news. But there was no murder, not unless you count suicide as a form of self-murder. Neil Cannery could never be paroled and committed suicide. Hanged himself in his cell as he listened to 'Death' by Judas Priest.

'Good riddance,' I said. 'I hope he rots in hell. Now let's listen to some classical music and see if we can wash away the horror of that metal maniac. Those bands have got a lot to answer for with those sorts of lyrics.'

Sue laughed, saying, 'Don't be silly. Our children listened to those songs, as do millions of others, and they lead normal lives.'

'I suppose so,' I grudgingly agreed. 'Even so, let's have a bit of Mozart, shall we?'

13: Cute Little Jinx

The Chosen One told me he has nothing against dumb animals, however sickeningly cute they are. 'Even Adolf loved his dogs,' he said to me one day. This conversation was about a million years after his fall from grace. 'And I have the most fantastically evil plan.'

I grinned. If Satan doesn't know how to truly unsettle the mortals, no one does. Which is how I, Beelzebub, Lord of the Flies, and second in command to the Grand Master of Evil, came to be searching a stray dogs' home for the cutest little puppy in the United Kingdom.

'Why the UK?' I asked my master before embarking on this deliciously degenerate adventure.

'Because,' he replied with that self-satisfied smile of malignant pleasure I adore, 'in many other parts of the world there is mayhem, death and destruction. I set those wheels in motion and those wheels will continue to turn for many years. But in the UK, it hasn't gone unnoticed – apart from a greedy and proud minority – that the natives behave in tolerant ways. And it is a nation of animal lovers. Especially dogs. With your help, perhaps we can change all that. Now it is time to unleash my master plan and show those jam-making goody-goodies how I can turn unconditional love upside down. By the time I'm through with them, they will never trust another pet.'

I left him laughing his head off as I dissolved into a destructive force, an unholy spirit to destabilize those pet-loving plaster saints.

The dogs' home I chose was on the periphery of a small home counties town. I examined the dogs carefully, weaving in and out of their cages, searching for a dog that would set the hardest hearts aflutter. Of course, I could not be seen. I am invisible. Always have been. Evil has a way of hiding, camouflaged in the commonplace in mortals' lives. But the dogs seemed possessed of a sixth sense, an instinct. Many of them shrank away from me, growling with distrust, as if they could smell my evil. But not possessed of a consciousness, they could not rationalise their fear, and couldn't work out what upset them so much.

I saw many mongrels, scruffy ill-treated and abandoned. There was rather a forlorn-looking King Charles Spaniel I thought might be taken up by a caring family. Another possibility was a sleek greyhound with warm, friendly eyes, crying out to be loved. But none of them was what I was looking for. I needed to find the one dog everyone wanted to love.

And then an adorable little scamp was brought in. He was very young, probably little more than a puppy. And I saw how the staff of the home responded. They were smitten. One of them bent down and tickled him behind the ears, stroked him sensually and drooled loving, sentimental words of gushing kindness. He had big brown eyes, cute floppy ears, and a tail that couldn't stop wagging its love and pleasure. I had found my cutie. This was the one.

Once the staff had departed it was time for me to take this mutt in hand, and I slid into his cage. As soon as he felt me approaching, he cringed back into the wall, his eyes pleading for mercy. I didn't rush things. Slowly, I let him get used to my evil scent. Eventually he became calm, and I muttered incantations, putting a diabolical spell on him. It worked. He began wagging his tail furiously. Our alliance was formed. An evil now bound us together for eternity. Soon the creature was jinxed, ready to commit the greatest atrocities this side of hell. And heaven help the first person or family who adopts him, I thought. No sooner had I revelled in this succulent idea than one of the staff returned with a young married couple and their seven-year-old daughter. As soon as they set eyes on the puppy, they all cooed and clucked their pleasure and the little girl squealed in delight. They adopted him, and I congratulated myself on a job well done.

Now it was time for me to follow this family and see how Jinx – which was my pet name for him – committed his first abomination.

They called him Timmy, and he settled down in their semi-detached home. Life seemed perfect, and their Timmy became an important part of the family. It was then I began to have doubts. Had my spell worked? Jinx seemed so content and loving with his new family, I couldn't imagine him harming them in any way.

Weeks passed, and still the little mutt showed no signs of becoming a demon of doom. I was disappointed. I had imagined the little fellow turning into a wild beast and savaging the little girl. But I soon discovered my Jinx was subtler than that.

It happened during a family outing. Dad was driving, with Mum in the front passenger seat, and the little girl in the back, cuddling her Timmy. The dog was over excited, and Dad asked her to keep him still. She held him tight, but he wriggled in her arms. We turned on to the motorway – I say 'we' because my evil spirit was there in the back with the child and Jinx. I could have sworn the dog stared at me, and I detected an animal cruelty in his eyes, the sort that domestic cats get as they relish torturing their prey. I knew just then he was no longer the lovable warm puppy he appeared. He belonged to us now and was tainted by the powers of evil. And what was so outstandingly great about his conversion is the fact that, as far as the little girl knew, he looked like the personification of innocence with those charming, warm, puppy dog eyes.

As we tore along the inside lane of the motorway, he suddenly began squirming in the girl's arms, then started barking loudly.

'Keep him quiet, Carla,' her father said, and at that moment he lost concentration and turned to look round. He was driving too fast, and in front of us a lorry had broken down in the slow lane. The accident was fantastic. Jinx did us proud.

The lorry had an open back and was stacked with sheets of corrugated iron and steel poles. As the car hit the rear of the lorry at 70 miles per hour, the entire front of the car seemed to disintegrate with a tearing of metal and splintering of glass. The corrugated iron decapitated the mother and father, and a steel pole rammed into the daughter's head, killing her instantly.

Naturally, Jinx survived the accident. And when the Fire and Accident crew arrived on the scene and saw this cute little puppy dog gazing at them with sweetness and light with his big brown eyes, pleading for them to get him out of there, and wagging his tail in a beseeching and appealing manner, they quickly got the metal-cutting equipment out and began cutting through the wreck.

One of the firemen I noticed was immediately besotted by Jinx. It looked like love at first sight. He only had eyes for the dog. His sympathy and pity centred on the surviving dumb animal, instead of the human passengers whose blood and entrails were splattered all over the car. As soon as the fire crew made a space big enough in the crushed wreck, Jinx was held and tugged through the aperture. He licked the fireman's face, showing his rescuer how grateful and loving he was, and what a loyal and splendid pet he could become.

I saw another adoption looming for our orphaned animal.

When I bragged about this splendid killing to Lucifer, he shrugged and said, 'One lump of coal does not a hellfire make.'

I took his point and returned to see how the fireman, whose name was Barry, was getting on with Jinx, who was now known as Lucky, because of his survival of the accident.

Lucky, I thought. Lucky for whom? Not for fireman Barry, that was for sure.

Barry was so in love with Lucky, they became inseparable. They went everywhere together. And the others in the fire crew were so bowled over by the little dog, he was accepted as their mascot, and sat in the fire engine's cab whenever they were called out on an emergency.

Lucky behaved perfectly, sat as good as gold in the fire engine, until one night they were called out to an empty warehouse that blazed. As the fire crew unwound the hoses, no one had bothered to close the door of the cab, because up until this emergency Lucky had always been on his best behaviour.

As the building burned, a large wooden door collapsed. Lucky bounded from the cab and into the warehouse.

'Lucky!' Barry screamed. 'What are you doing? Here boy! Come back here!'

But our Jinx had gone into the heart of the blaze. The fire crew tried to restrain Barry, stop him from following to attempt a rescue. But Barry broke away from his colleagues and bravely followed his dog into the blazing building. Of course, his mask protected him from smoke inhalation, but it was an old building, and the heavy wooden flooring above gave way and fell on Barry, pinning him to the ground. He peered through the smoke, seeing if he could see his precious pet, and caught sight of lucky, staring at him through the thick fumes. What amazed Barry in his final moments was the way the dog seemed able to survive the smoke and heat. The last thing Barry saw was Lucky scampering quickly towards the rear of the building where he escaped through another collapsed door.

Barry perished in the fire.

Satan was pleased with the result. 'Now we're getting somewhere,' he told me. 'But I want those mortals to fear owning the dog. I want them to know how much evil and bad luck he could bring them.'

'After what happened at the warehouse conflagration, none of the others in the fire crew were willing to adopt Lucky,' I assured the Chosen One. 'They regarded their mascot as a risk.'

Satan burst into that full-throttle laugh of his, and his eyes filled with malicious glee. 'We must have more mayhem,' he screamed. 'Bring it on, Beelzebub.'

'Your wish is my command, O Master,' I said, bowing.

'What? You think you're some fucking genii now? Just get on with it.'

The news of the fire, and Jinx's erratic behaviour, the way he caused the death of a respected fireman, was reported in the national newspapers. Now there was a certain reluctance to adopt him, and he was taken in by the R.S.P.C.A. for a while. But he wasn't with them for long. His picture in the paper had melted the heart of recently retired widow, Mrs Lucy Lavery, who missed her husband, and thought Lucky was the perfect solution to her loneliness. She made a home for him, near the seaside, and he sat obediently at her feet each night, biding his time.

The time came less than a month later as she took him out for his daily routine. It was a clifftop walk, a narrow path a good ten or more feet back from the chalk cliffs. There were warnings not to go near the edge of the cliff as it was considered dangerous and liable to crumble. The drop was a good hundred feet on to jagged rocks below. I could guess at what Jinx was planning as he got accustomed to the area, sniffing his way along the clifftop walk, cocking his leg up every so often as he surveyed the terrain. Every so often he wandered close to the cliff edge, and Mrs Lavery would admonish him.

'Lucky! Come away from there. There's a good dog. Come here! Do as you're told.'

All of which he ignored of course as he searched for the perfect drop. And then, early one morning as they took their usual constitutional, and neared the spot Lucky had reconnoitred, he suddenly barked as if he had seen a rabbit, ran to the cliff edge and jumped over. Mrs Lavery gasped in horror and ran after him, hoping to save him. But Lucky knew of a narrow ledge hidden beneath the overhang of the clifftop. As he lay on the ledge, he watched Mrs Lavery sail over the crumbling edge of the cliff and fly swiftly to her death on the rocks.

I was so proud of my furry acolyte. My Angel of Death was just getting into his stride.

Having climbed back to the edge of the cliff, he peered over and barked furiously. His barking soon drew the attention of several walkers. People flocked to the beach below to see the dramatic spectacle of Mrs Lavery's demise, her shattered brains spilling blood and gore into a rock pool. Along with the police came the local vicar. Mrs Lavery had been an avid churchgoer, and the vicar, the Reverend Tombs, prayed for her departed soul. And knowing how much she had loved that dog, Reverend Tombs agreed to look after him until a suitable home could be found.

This was better than I could have hoped for. If Jinx could destroy a man of the cloth, then Satan would be overcome with self-esteem and pride.

Less than a week went by when the vicar popped into the church one Wednesday to see how the restoration was coming on. There was scaffolding just beyond the pulpit, covering the altar, as the stained glass window behind had been damaged in a freak storm and was being repaired. A giant brass cross was soon to be suspended over the altar and lay on a plank on the top of the scaffolding. The workmen had gone to lunch when Reverend Tombs entered with Lucky on a lead. The vicar sat the dog down in the nave, near the front pew, while he went to examine work on the stained glass window. He stood below the scaffolding, peering through the slats. He had his hand on one of the upright poles, which shook slightly. His back was to Lucky, so he didn't see the intense stare of the dog, who focused on the brass cross at the top of the scaffolding. Suddenly, the Reverend Tombs lost his balance and grabbed the pole to stop himself from falling over. The top plank shook, the brass cross was dislodged, and it fell from the plank, observed dispassionately by Lucky. The cross was solid and heavy, made doubly so by its momentum, and the long end landed directly in the middle of Tombs' head, cracking it open like a boiled egg.

My four-legged fiend had excelled himself.

Now people started to notice a link between Jinx and his owners meeting an untimely death. It was now suggested there was a jinx on Jinx.

But that didn't deter some other foolhardy mortals who couldn't resist that cute little laughing face, tongue lolling cheekily, and those velvety floppy ears. Next in line was a bus driver, whose friend was looking after Lucky and took him on the bus. There were thirteen people killed in that crash. Of course, Lucky came out of it unscathed, and wagging his tail.

Three more unlucky Lucky owners met an untimely death until a journalist investigating the events came up with the headlining story: DOG OF DOOM. Now nobody wanted Lucky. Someone suggested he was so unlucky he should be put to sleep. But there was a hue and cry from animal lovers everywhere. And so Jinx was taken back into care. Looked after by the R.S.P.C.A.

It looked as if the my hellhound's rampant death toll might be curtailed. Then I was astounded when an elderly couple applied to the animal pound for custody of Jinx. Of course, R.S.P.C.A. staff warned them of his history, laying it on thick.

But the couple, a man in his mid-seventies, and his wife, a few years younger, protested that they were not superstitious. In fact, they said, they were atheists, and they didn't believe that drivel about an animal being jinxed, and suggested the deaths might be no more than coincidence, accidents that may have happened anyway.

They got custody of Jinx. Now, I thought, we'll see who's right about the curse.

But as the years dragged by, nothing happened. Jinx died of old age when he was 14-years-old. I was furious, livid that the elderly couple outlived my cursed dog.

'Maybe the curse wore off,' I explained to Satan. 'It needed to be recharged.'

The Chosen One smiled knowingly. 'Nothing we could have done about it. You see, they were non-believers, and therefore immune from the curse.'

I was incensed and felt like tempting a super-power president into pushing the nuclear button.

'You see,' said Lucifer arrogantly. 'Nothing we can do about the atheists.'

'Atheists,' I sneered. 'Bugger them. They ruin everything.'

You may also enjoy...

PLEASE SIR!

THE OFFICIAL HISTORY

DAVID BARRY

Lightning Source UK Ltd.
Milton Keynes UK
UKHW011835111221
395488UK00001B/77